DATE DUE			

The Unmaking of Duncan Veerick

Betty Levin

Front Street
Asheville, North Carolina

For David and Mary Alice

Copyright © 2007 by Betty Levin
All rights reserved
Printed in China
Designed by Helen Robinson
First edition

Library of Congress Cataloging-in-Publication Data
Levin, Betty.
The unmaking of Duncan Veerick / Betty Levin.—1st ed.
p. cm.
Summary: Reluctantly, thirteen-year-old Duncan helps his neighbor,
a widow recovering from a stroke, by hiding valuable antiques and art
objects her husband had collected, but disaster strikes and the secrets he has been
asked to keep may mean big trouble for Duncan.
ISBN-13: 978-1-932425-96-3 (hardcover : alk. paper)
[1. Collectors and collecting—Fiction. 2. Neighborliness—Fiction.
3. Old age—Fiction. 4. People with disabilities—Fiction.
5. Swindlers and swindling—Fiction. 6. Dogs—Fiction.] I. Title.
PZ7.L5759Unm 2007
[Fic]—dc22   2006101747

Front Street
An Imprint of Boyds Mills Press, Inc.
815 Church Street
Honesdale, Pennsylvania 18431

We live, not by things, but by the meanings
of things. It is needful to transmit the passwords
from generation to generation.
—*Antoine de Saint-Exupéry*

For the longest time Duncan didn't get it. Once he began to realize how he'd messed up, he still wasn't careful enough when their questions came at him.

They asked him to begin at the beginning, leaving nothing out.

"Take your time," they advised, sounding patient, understanding. "Consider how you account for yourself," they urged while he offered up useless details or corrected some insignificant time sequence.

He barely heard their altered tone.

Finally one of them said, "Maybe you didn't plan to take advantage of the situation when Astrid Valentine welcomed you into her home."

He heard that. It finally sank in. He was a suspect.

Starting over, he thought back to the blustery January afternoon when that silly little dog bounced across Garnet Road and Astrid Valentine came lumbering after it.

"Come back, Mo!" she'd howled, her slippers flapping and her massive arms flailing. "Mo! You bad boy! Come!" That was when she'd caught sight of Duncan walking home from the school bus. "Help!" she'd called to him. By then she was gulping huge breaths that sounded like sobs. "Oh, catch him! He'll be run over."

There wasn't a car in sight, although you could hear traffic down on the highway. Duncan had glanced back hoping that Tracy Mattos would come forward to deal with Mrs. Valentine. But Tracy had already turned in at her driveway, and he was on his own.

So Duncan had lowered his backpack and crouched in time to catch the dog as it hurled itself at him. When he carried the wiggly creature over to Mrs. Valentine, she clasped it so hard that it yelped. Before she turned and waddled back toward her open front door, she'd said, "He doesn't usually bolt like that. He has his own door into the back yard where it's fenced and safe. I don't know what came over him."

Duncan had nodded as he retrieved his backpack. He'd never had anything to say to Mrs. Valentine, especially after that Halloween years ago when their older sisters had dressed him and Tracy up and sent them trick-or-treating to the only other house on Garnet Road. Mrs. Valentine had left them standing on the front step while she picked up the dog and went off to find a treat. When she'd finally reappeared with two Fig Newtons, they just gaped at them until she said, "They're not poisoned, you know." They'd taken the offering, mumbled their thanks, and fled. The Fig Newtons were stale, hard as rocks.

They got the message and steered clear of the Valentine house after that.

The questions hammered harder. "When did you begin to culti-vate a relationship with Mrs. Valentine?" they asked. "To gain her trust?"

By now he understood what they were getting at. They already knew that he had wormed his way in through the dog door that time she locked herself out of her house. He still couldn't shake off a remnant of embarrassment from that incident, even though no one had seen him half stuck, the little dog hysterically pawing at his head and face and licking him blind. By the time he'd dragged himself inside and made his way to the front door to let Mrs. Valentine in, her embarrassment momentarily eclipsed his own.

He told the social worker that he supposed that was the real beginning. It was why he hadn't mentioned the time when the little dog had escaped.

But when she treated that slip like a deliberate omission, everything that followed seemed loaded, especially when he heard himself admitting how much he'd resented being at Astrid's beck and call.

And then the bone fragments were found, unearthed in the rubble. Human bones. After that discovery, the inquiry shifted into high gear, altering the tone and force and direction of their questions. Even then Duncan assumed that all he had to do was set them straight. But it wasn't that simple. What he knew didn't seem to interest them nearly so much as the fact that he hadn't leveled with them from the start.

So what did they want from him? He could still talk about how he and Astrid had been thrown together because of the dog. But what really mattered, the music, was something else. How could he explain it to people who called friendship dependency? Because, yes, in spite of everything, what had sprung up between them was a kind of friendship. At least as much as a fat old woman and a skinny thirteen-year-old kid who was into rock climbing could become friends.

"Take your time," they said. "Say what's on your mind. Help us understand."

Duncan started over. He would recall everything he could. Voices most of all. Sights and smells and sounds, both close and distant. Traffic way down on the highway. Cows at the Mattos barn lowing as they waited to be milked or fed or both. Winter crows in search of roadkill or hapless chipmunks. The slap and clatter of dinner hurriedly prepared because his parents had gotten home late again. Hamburgers sizzling on the stove. The telephone ringing, his sister Roz dashing to pick it up.

She handed the phone to her mother, saying, "It's Mrs. Valentine."

Duncan hadn't yet mentioned finding her locked out on this frigid winter afternoon. Now he could tell from his mother's side of the conversation that she was learning that once again he'd come to Mrs. Valentine's aid. Mom kept saying, "Oh!" and "Oh, really?" She reached for the spatula and gestured for the hamburgers to be flipped.

When they were sitting around the kitchen table, Duncan's good deed was served up with the meal.

Roz was the first of them to react. "Another reason for cell phone service. Anyhow, shouldn't she have an alarm system so she won't need a key if she locks herself out?"

Mom nodded. "That would work if all Astrid forgets are keys. What if she forgets her code?"

"Oh, right," said Roz. "I didn't think of that." She glanced at her brother and said, "I promise not to tell any of my friends how you broke in." She giggled. "But I wish I'd been there. With a camera," she added. Duncan kicked her under the table.

Their father said, "Knock it off, you two. Small acts of kindness are rare enough these days."

"Small is right," Roz retorted. "If Duncan was any bigger, he might still be there, halfway in and halfway out."

Dad couldn't suppress his own grin. They all laughed, Duncan included. As long as Roz kept her word and no one else heard about it, he could afford to treat it as a joke.

But there was nothing funny about the next crisis. It was Sunday morning, and everyone was lolling around waiting for the day to start. Roz had hunkered down with the phone in the coat closet to talk to her boyfriend Denny when a sudden pounding on the front door brought Duncan's parents to their feet.

There was Doris Beasley, distraught and breathless. "Something terrible's happened!" she gasped. "I called the Mattos farm, but Wanda's at church already. When I tried you, your line was busy. It's Astrid. She's lying on the floor and she's talking funny. She won't let me call 911 till she's cleaned up. See, she dirtied herself. She's a mess. I feel so bad. Usually I look in on her Saturday mornings and do her shopping and then, you know, tidy up for her. But I couldn't make it yesterday."

Mom said, "She'll need a doctor. An ambulance."

"She won't let anyone see her this way, but she's too heavy for me to lift by myself."

"I'll come," Dad said.

But Doris Beasley threw up a hand. "No men," she said.

"Just to help get her off the floor," Mom explained.

"Not the way she is. After she's cleaned. You come, Natalie," Doris Beasley said to Mom. "We can manage together to make her more presentable."

Mom said, "I'm not sure it makes sense to worry about appearances at a time like this." She called through the closet door, "Roz! You come too. Roz! Get off the phone!"

"I'll send for an ambulance," said Dad.

"Not yet," Doris told him. "We'll call from her house after she's done."

"Done," muttered Dad, turning away from the front door and shaking his head.

Mom and Roz went off to the Valentine house with Doris Beasley.

Nearly an hour later Roz returned alone.

"Everything all right?" asked Dad.

Roz shook her head. "It's gross," she said. "I've never seen or smelled anything so gross." She headed upstairs.

"Was Mrs. Valentine conscious?" Dad called after her.

"Sort of. I guess so." Roz turned midway and said to Duncan, "You don't know how lucky you are to be male and unwanted over there."

"No need to take it out on your brother," Dad said to her. "Even if it was unpleasant. Being helpful isn't always a joy ride."

"Tell me!" she flung back. She pounded up the remaining steps, and a moment later they heard the shower turned on full force.

Even though Duncan became expert at anticipating many of their repeated questions, that didn't mean he could provide satisfactory answers. Take the one that went, "At what point did you start going into the Valentine house on your own, and how often did you go there?"

As little as possible, Duncan could have told them, remembering his resistance to being dragged into the dog-tending arrangement. He had known Roz would prevail against his arguments. Of course she reminded their parents of her own middle school years of servitude, "sitting" for Duncan every weekday afternoon. Now in high school, she was making up for lost opportunities in after-school activities. Besides, the little dog already knew Duncan.

He fought hard, though, pointing out that Roz had helped rescue the dog when she helped rescue Mrs. Valentine. But his argument crumbled because Doris Beasley had locked the dog out in the yard while they attended to Mrs. Valentine. Roz had heard it yapping out there. Then Duncan tried another tack, bringing up Mr. Simon, who came to Chiswick Middle School just one day a week and was giving him extra trumpet lessons so he'd get into the band when he started high school.

Roz shook her head. "You don't want to be a band geek," she informed him, neatly changing the subject. "All the kids that can't do anything else end up in the band."

Duncan resigned himself to being the weekday dog tender. Doris Beasley would keep it with her on weekends.

"Consider what you're doing like an after-school job," Roz suggested. "Maybe Mrs. Valentine will pay you when she gets home."

"Consider it being a good neighbor," Mom said. "It won't kill you to help out in a crisis. The way Roz did," she added.

Duncan didn't miss the smugness that canceled out his sister's grimace of disgust at their mother's reminder. But Roz couldn't resist adding, "At least the dog won't smell like—"

"Roz," Mom said, "that's enough. Instead of dwelling on all that, think what it must have been like for that poor woman lying helpless for who knows how long all alone."

Duncan sent Roz a look that meant he wasn't finished with this latest unfairness. She returned his silent message with an infuriating smile.

"Doris Beasley finally got in touch with Astrid's nephew," Mom continued. "He's coming next weekend. Doris is getting him a room in Brixton. Meanwhile, she hopes to be with Astrid at the hospital most days after work. That's why we're going to see to the dog."

We, thought Duncan, fingering Mrs. Valentine's house key in his pocket. Easy for you to say.

Monday after school when he entered the house the little dog hurled itself at him with a kind of desperation that might have seemed pitiful if the dog had come to its senses after a while and calmed down. But it continued to race around, yapping shrilly and clawing everything it came in contact with—floor, chair, his pants, the door.

As soon as Duncan managed to shove the dog through the flap door to the back yard, it popped right back in again. Duncan went out and walked it along the fenced boundary. Beyond the fence and propped against a long shed was the sign that used to hang at the road end of the driveway. Although it was splotched with snow, he could read the large words:

VALENTINE SALVAGE —FIXTURES

Once there had been an enormous faucet above it. When he was little he thought it was real, imagining a kitchen fit for a giant, until someone told him it was only painted plywood. As he studied the sign, he began to make out faded markings that overlay the big words. And a few dark spots. Bullet holes. The faded markings were the remains of a crude peace sign someone had painted over the still-bold words.

Duncan wasn't clear on what led to the shooting, only that afterward it became common knowledge that Mace Mattos had done it. Had he hit the enormous faucet as well? Duncan couldn't remember. Nothing remained to direct salvage seekers to their destination but a few old iron stoves that were ranged along the far side of the snowy, weed-clogged driveway. They faced the yard like fossilized spectators waiting for a show, a game, or maybe just relief from boredom.

Making his way back inside through the people door, Duncan found Doris Beasley's instructions in the kitchen beside a dog dish. He filled the water bowl and found the dog food on the landing at the top of the cellar stairs. He put the dish of food on the floor beside the water bowl, but the dog ignored it. Instead it clawed at him beseechingly.

"All right," he told it. "I'll stay a little longer."

Aimlessly he wandered across the hall into the living room.

It felt strange, as if the room itself were conscious of his uninvited presence. He looked at the soiled and hairy couch covered with cushions and blankets. The dog scrambled up on it, rooted around, and came flying over to Duncan with a knotted sock in its mouth. It shook the sock violently and thrust it at Duncan, who wouldn't touch it.

He wouldn't touch anything in this overstuffed room. He wasn't here to snoop either. He was just passing time to make the dog feel less lonely.

Despite windows on facing walls, the room seemed dark and airless. In Duncan's house the living room was light and airy. Here, across from where he stood, the long wall was all shelves, some of them crammed with books, some holding objects he couldn't identify. And there were photographs, too, sort of all mixed up with the unrecognizable objects. There were more photographs on the desk beside him. On the table between the windows were stacks of folders, a bowl, and some bone things that were made to look like people and animals. Weird.

As he turned to leave, one of the desk photos caught his attention. It showed a woman in a long dress holding a cigarette in one hand, a microphone in the other. Some celebrity, he figured. Someone Astrid Valentine admired from a long time ago.

Back in the front hall, he paused. Should he take the dog into the kitchen again and show it the food in the dish?

No. He'd already spent nearly an hour here. He told the dog he'd be back tomorrow, ducked out the front door, and headed home.

It was a relief to be out of that house.

"What do you do in there?" Tracy Mattos asked Duncan as they walked down to the highway.

"In where?" He knew what she meant. He just didn't want her talking about it, especially not on the bus or in school.

Roz, who sometimes walked with them, said, "You know. In the Valentine house. Which," she added, "is no valentine."

Tracy turned to her. "How come?"

Duncan shot his sister a warning look. Their parents had made it clear that they shouldn't blab about Astrid Valentine's predicament.

Roz shrugged. "Well, the only time I was there, well ... I guess you can't tell much, really. We were totally busy with Mrs. Valentine."

Tracy said, "My mother and father used to go over there when Mr. Valentine was alive. But the Chicken Lady didn't like kids, so they never took me or my sisters." Tracy called Mrs. Valentine the Chicken Lady even though she didn't keep chickens anymore. "All Mom ever said was that the Valentine place wasn't like any other house she knew. Now Doris Beasley sort of helps out there."

Duncan nodded.

"Well, what's it like, Duncan? What do you do there?"

"Feed the dog," Duncan told her, peering down the highway for the bus.

"Why don't you just take it home with you until she's back?" Tracy asked.

"No one's in our house all day," Roz said.

"It's used to its own place," added Duncan. "The back yard's fenced."

"It came down to the farm once," Tracy said. "Barked at the cows. Barked at our dog. Dad said it didn't have an ounce of sense, but Mom called it a mop with a mouth. She told us that inside that dirty gray mop with a mouth was a frustrated watchdog or ratter. But you know what my sister Darlene said? She was still living here then."

Duncan wasn't really interested in what Darlene Mattos had to say about the dog, but he didn't know how to halt the torrent of words. Although Tracy was a year behind him in school, she was a head taller and a whole lot heavier. Stronger, too, he suspected from the way she could sling the square hay bales. As far as he could tell, she was a loner who spent most of her spare time in front of the television. Even without other kids on Garnet Road, they tended to go their separate ways.

Now he saw with relief that their bus was in sight, the bus for the regional high school just behind it.

"My sister Darlene says the dog is, like, instead of a cat that goes with a witch. I forget what that's called."

"A familiar," said Roz, laughing as she went off to her bus.

Duncan and Tracy got on theirs and headed for seats far apart, as they always did.

Once he was in school, Duncan didn't give Tracy or the Valentine dog another thought. But that afternoon when the bus dropped Duncan and Tracy off at the foot of Garnet Road, she fell into step beside him. She started out silent. Then she said, "If you want to work at the farm this summer, you'd better talk to my mom. She's signing kids up already."

Duncan nodded. Then he said, "I might not be able to if Mrs. Valentine stays away."

"You get paid for taking care of the dog?"

He said, "I don't know. It's still an emergency."

She cast an appraising look his way and shook her head.

Annoyed, he said, "When she comes home, then she'll settle up. If she can."

Tracy nodded. "Meanwhile you've got a place to go to that's, like, all your own."

Duncan, who hadn't thought of it that way, said, "I guess." What did she think he went to every afternoon at home? But she must be thinking of her own situation. There was always somebody at the farm.

He slowed as they came to her driveway. But Tracy crossed the road and walked on until they were abreast of the Valentine house. She gazed up at its weathered clapboards and peeling paint beneath the steeply gabled roof that was designed to shed snow.

"You going in now?" Tracy asked.

He nodded. "The dog's been alone all day."

She stopped. "Can I come with you?"

Duncan had a feeling she shouldn't, not without permission. But permission from whom? Anyway, what harm could it do? He shrugged. "I guess," he answered reluctantly.

The dog tore at the door, yapping furiously, as Duncan worked the key in the lock. He had to swing his backpack at the dog to keep it from dashing out to the road when he got the door open.

Once inside, he knew he should try to calm it down, but he just stood in the front hall while the dog whirled around and around, until Tracy broke away and moved into the kitchen.

The dog scampered after her, still yapping.

As Duncan slowly followed, Tracy reached for the refrigerator door.

"Hey, don't," Duncan told her.

She turned, surprised. "Why not? What's in there?"

"I don't know," he said. "But it's not … It's hers."

"But what if there's stuff rotting in there?"

"There wouldn't be. Doris Beasley would take care of it."

"I bet she left a snack for you, then. Aren't you hungry?"

He shook his head. Sure, he was hungry, but he'd get something to eat later at home.

"Well, I am," Tracy declared, pulling open the refrigerator door.

Duncan kept his distance, but he couldn't help glancing at the white interior, where there was a can of something and part of a chocolate bar and nothing else.

"Close it," he ordered as Tracy reached for the chocolate. "It's not ours. We weren't invited."

"Man, you're uptight," Tracy said with disgust. "In my house you'd be welcome to anything that wasn't, you know, whole."

"Well, we're not in your house. If you're so hungry—"

"Okay, okay. Cool it, Duncan. Let's see what else there is." She strode back through the front hall and into the living room.

He called out pointedly, "I'm taking the dog to the yard." When he opened the back door, the little dog came flying past him. Outside, it dashed around in aimless frenzy. Duncan figured that all he had to do was stand still to make it think they were playing together. Maybe if he kept it company like this for a while, Tracy would get bored and leave.

Eventually the dog ran out of steam and went off to roll in the snow. Duncan gave it a few more minutes before he went back inside.

From the kitchen it sounded as though someone else had come in. Then he realized that Tracy was talking to herself. That figured, he thought. Maybe craziness ran in the family. Plenty of people said Tracy's uncle Mace was unhinged because of Vietnam.

"Time to go," Duncan called from the kitchen.

Tracy met him in the hall. "Seen this?" she exclaimed. She held up an antique lantern.

"Put it back!" Duncan ordered.

"I'm just, like, appreciating," she told him.

"Well, don't," he snapped. "Unless you're invited to."

She grinned at him. "So invite me."

"No. I can't. I shouldn't even let anyone in."

Tracy shrugged and walked back into the living room, where she deposited the lantern on a small table. "I'm glad I don't have to dust all this stuff," she remarked.

"Come on," he said. "Let's get out of here."

But she took her time. He went outside to wait on the broad granite step in front of the door. Just as she finally emerged from the house and he locked the door behind her, a car slowed and Roz called to him, "Want a lift?"

Denny, who was driving, said, "Hi, Duncan. Tracy, right? Hi."

Duncan got in back. Tracy watched him climb in, then crossed the street to the farm.

Roz didn't say anything. Not then. After they got home and Duncan got out, she stayed with Denny in his car the way she usually did, but this time not for long.

"What were you two up to?" she demanded before she had even slammed the front door.

Duncan, on his way upstairs, paused. "Nothing. What do you mean?"

"Tracy Mattos in Mrs. Valentine's house with you?"

"Most of the time I was out in the back yard with the dog. What's the big deal?"

"You know. Tracy's kind of, well, you know."

He turned to look at Roz. "No, I don't know. Fat? Clueless? What?"

Roz shook her head. "You just don't get it. Everyone in Chiswick's going to hear about you two alone there."

"So what?" Duncan demanded. "She's a neighbor. She stopped in for a few minutes."

"Great!" Roz groaned. "Hanging out with a loser."

What was this really about? Not Mrs. Valentine's house, he guessed. Not his image, if there could be such a thing. Only how it would reflect on Roz. All of a sudden resentment rose up, and he blurted, "You want to take care of that dog and protect the house and all? Fine. I'll do mornings. You do afternoons. Then you can shut out whoever you want."

"You know I can't," Roz snapped back. Then she softened. "I know it's no picnic, Duncan. But it's only for a little while. When Mrs. Valentine gets home, you'll be off the hook."

He nodded glumly. Then, while she was still sounding sympathetic, he made one more stab at getting her to help. "At least Wednesday afternoons? I'm missing band practice. See, it was all arranged. I was going to go to Neil's house afterward until Mom and Dad picked me up."

"You know I can't. Wednesdays I don't get home till supper-time. You'll see when you're in high school next year. You'll be into a bunch of after-school stuff. Anyway, consider what you're doing now useful experience. Besides all the Brownie points. Didn't you hear Dad say that what you're doing goes above and beyond the call of duty?"

"There's nothing to do there," Duncan burst out.

"Well, just think of how proud Dad is of you. So I guess if you have a dorky friend over once in a while—"

"Tracy's not a friend!" he protested. "She's just a neighbor. Same as Mrs. Valentine."

"I get your point," Roz told him. "Anyway, if you do have her over, take her out back with the dog instead of inside."

He shrugged. He wasn't about to admit how uncomfortable he'd been with Tracy in that house.

Duncan settled into a routine. He fed the dog in the morning, quickly. When he fed it again in the afternoon, he took extra time to be outside with it. He tried everything he could think of to get it to play games, but the little dog refused to fetch, and it treated tug-of-war as an invitation to bite at his boots or jeans.

Weekends were a relief. Not that he did much with them. He just felt the expansiveness of Saturday and Sunday and steered clear of the Valentine house when he walked down to the highway to meet Neil.

One evening midweek when they were cleaning up after supper, his mother mentioned that Astrid Valentine was being released from the hospital and would be moved to the rehab center in Woodford.

Dad said, "Maybe you should visit her."

Mom nodded. "Maybe both of us should." She turned to Duncan. "Do you want to come with us? You could tell her about the dog."

"No way!" he retorted.

"Duncan!" Mom exclaimed. "What's the matter with you?"

He didn't answer.

Mom said, "She can't help it that she needs someone to care for her pet."

"I know," Duncan said.

His mother and father decided to drive over to Woodford the next day on their lunch breaks. Duncan heaved a sigh. At least it was during school, which meant he wasn't available.

That Friday morning he found a note from Doris Beasley next to the dog food. It said that Astrid's nephew was coming to see her again, and this time he would be staying in the house through the weekend. Mo would have to be shut in the kitchen. Otherwise he might escape out the front door, as the nephew wasn't very careful with dogs.

Since the note didn't mention exactly when the nephew was coming, Duncan shut Mo in the kitchen before he left for school.

That afternoon Tracy came with him all the way to the house again. "Mrs. Valentine's nephew might be here," he told her.

Tracy said, "I'll meet you out back."

There was no car nearby. Nor was there any sign of a new arrival in the front hall, although that didn't mean much. If the nephew was here, he'd have taken his stuff upstairs to the spare room. But the dog, Mo, was still shut in the kitchen. Released, he greeted Duncan hysterically, darting out the dog door and back inside, over and over until Duncan let himself out the regular door into the yard.

Tracy was already standing at the gate. She waited for the dog to calm down before telling Duncan the bolt was rusted shut. He was about to tell her to climb over when she turned away and headed for the small door beside the closed loading entrance at the end of the shed.

"What are you doing?" he called to her.

"I'm going to get something to stand on so I can come into the yard."

"You can't … ," he began, but she was unstoppable.

The padlock on the door didn't faze her. She picked up a rusty nail and inserted it into the keyhole. When the nail broke off, she twisted and yanked the lock to shake the stuck nail loose. The lock mount, still attached to a splintered shaft of rotten doorjamb, pulled free. After that, she only had to wrench the door hard before it gave enough to allow her to squeeze through.

It seemed to Duncan that she took a long time inside finding something to stand on. After a while he stopped worrying about the nephew driving up to the house and began to feel uneasy in a new kind of way. Leaving Mo digging a snow hole, Duncan vaulted over the gate. He glanced around. He could see part of a chicken house and coop beyond the shed. There was nothing along the driveway with its derelict stoves.

Finally he peered through the open shed door. Tracy, halfway down the dim interior, was bending over one of the sheets of plywood propped on sawhorses that stretched end to end the length of the building. He could also see that each makeshift plywood table was covered with hundreds, maybe thousands, of doorknobs and latches. Here there were faucets and over there hinges and beyond those all kinds of light fixtures.

"Tracy? What are you doing?" He started toward her along the narrow corridor between the loaded tables.

"Looking," she replied. "Ever seen anything like this?" She held up an elaborate iron grate. "What do you suppose it's for?" Reaching across to pick up something else, she pressed against the plywood, which shifted away from her and tilted. Hinges and grates began to slide to the floor.

"Tracy!" Duncan yelled.

"Oops," she said, giggling.

Now would be the moment for the nephew to appear.

"It's not funny," he told her as he dove underneath to check the fall. "We're breaking and entering."

"No one's going to find us here. Anyway, who would care? Look at all this stuff."

It wasn't easy to hold up one end of the plywood while Tracy nudged the sawhorse back in place. Duncan stayed underneath to pick up the fallen pieces, all of them coated with dust. Finally he straightened. Now that his eyes had adjusted to the dim light, he could see what fascinated her. But he resisted touching anything else.

"I bet they're worth a lot," Tracy said.

"They're junk," he replied.

"I don't know … My dad said builders and even architects used to come here to buy off Mr. Valentine. Some wicked big deals. Think of it all going to waste."

"Well, there's no one to sell it. Especially now," Duncan added. "Now that Mrs. Valentine's had the stroke."

"When she gets home, we should offer to run a big yard sale for her. What do you think?"

"When she gets home," Duncan replied, "I'm out of here."

"I don't know," Tracy said again, following him to the door. "I bet you could make a lot more money selling this stuff than haying for my dad."

Duncan shrugged. All he could really think about right now was getting Tracy and himself outside and the mounted padlock stuck back on the doorjamb, at least looking as though it worked.

When Doris came to pick up the dog Friday evening, she stopped by to talk to Duncan's parents about what she called the "situation." "It's Astrid's nephew," she said. "He wants to get the house ready for her, and he asked me to help move everything, but he won't listen to me. Maybe you could tell him that Astrid likes her things left alone."

"We don't even know the guy," Dad said.

"Astrid might've asked him to do whatever he's planning," Mom suggested.

"She's … she's not ready to make decisions," Doris said. "When she comes home, she ought to find everything exactly the way it was. She should feel like it's her home."

"Of course she should," Mom agreed. "You know, she seemed all right when we saw her. Weak, but in good spirits. Probably her nephew's prepared her for changes."

Doris shook her head. "If he thinks he has, he doesn't know Astrid. I tried to tell him, but he thinks I'm just the cleaning lady."

"Oh, no!" Mom exclaimed. "Will he be here through the weekend? Maybe Rick could sort of check in to see if he needs any help."

Doris said, "What if you invite him over for a meal?"

Duncan's parents exchanged looks.

"He'd probably say no," Doris added quickly, "but it would give you an opening."

She was almost out the door before Mom realized they didn't even know the nephew's name. She asked.

"Shoop," Doris told them. "Eddie Shoop. Before this he used to visit her maybe once a year. He's her closest relative. He lives in New Jersey. He can't exactly drop in."

Duncan's father closed the door behind her, shook his head, and sighed.

Duncan said, "Want me to talk to him? I'll do that if you do the dog next week."

Dad said, "Knock it off, Duncan. You don't have to remind us about your neighborly efforts."

Mom said, "Still, he's got a point."

The phone rang and put an end to the discussion. Roz was calling to say she and a bunch of kids were going out for pizza. Denny would bring her home. Duncan knew that Roz's social life was of a lot more concern than Astrid Valentine's nephew.

Since he'd heard it all a million times, he went up to his room to get out of earshot. Homework didn't appeal to him, not with the whole weekend ahead. He flung himself down on the bed and stared at the ceiling, his thoughts adrift. Images of door handles, plumbing fixtures, grates, and other stuff not yet identified came and went.

Saturday morning Dad was on his way to the landfill when Eddie Shoop emerged from the Valentine house and walked down to the road. Dad pulled up, got out, and spoke to the nephew. Duncan, who was about to lug the empty trash bins back to the house, caught a glimpse of the encounter, brief as it was.

Afterward Dad said that Eddie Shoop appreciated the offer,

but the time for help would come when Astrid returned home. Thanks to the downstairs bathroom, that homecoming might be fairly soon. He was arranging to rent a hospital bed to be set up in the kitchen. And, yes, he realized Doris Beasley was a loyal friend to his aunt, but she was also one of those tiresome women who like to be in charge of everything. Well, he certainly didn't want to hurt her feelings. He'd do something to show his gratitude.

On Monday morning Duncan found another note from Doris Beasley at the Valentine house, this time beside a box of chocolates. "Help yourself," the note read. "Eddie Shoop left this. Nice of him, I suppose, but I'm a diabetic. Enjoy. Doris B."

Duncan looked around. The kitchen table was in the already crowded living room. The couch had been dragged away from the wall, exposing more shelves crammed with all sorts of things. These changes didn't seem to amount to much. Still, he couldn't help feeling that Doris Beasley must know what she was talking about. No wonder she resented the nephew. It was cool the way she dismissed his peace offering.

Mo, who had run out to the yard, came bounding back inside to make a wild sweep of the living room. Snatching up something small from the newly accessible bottom shelf, he went prancing off with it into the kitchen. Some long-lost toy, Duncan figured.

He walked past the couch and squatted down for a closer look at what were clearly not fixtures like doorknobs and faucet handles. Were those metal things horse bits? He couldn't be sure. There were several more bones like the ones on the small table. Or were they horns? Some of them were so pitted and rough he could hardly tell. Only they were more than bones or horns—they were crudely shaped into people and animals. And there were other figures made of polished stone.

Mo raced back through the hallway into the living room holding his prize high and shaking it, a clear challenge to Duncan. Halfheartedly he reached for a protruding part of it. Only as he seized it did he realize it wasn't a dog toy. It was one of those carved bone things.

He pried open Mo's jaws. The dog growled fiercely, playfully, but let the thing go. It certainly wasn't beautiful like the stone objects. But it had an arresting presence as if it had once possessed some meaning. Duncan set it out of Mo's reach and then watched the dog dive in to grab another one.

Duncan picked up all the figures he thought the dog might damage and stuck them on higher shelves wherever he could find space for them, a few alongside the books, most of the more elaborate ones tucked in behind them. It seemed like the only thing to do, or else Mo would have to be confined again, and Duncan wasn't about to do that to the frantic little dog.

Back in the kitchen he eyed the box of chocolates and reread Doris Beasley's note. Diabetic or not, she wasn't about to be bought off this way. First the nephew would have to treat her with proper respect. Duncan didn't blame her. Even after he caught a faint whiff of the chocolate, he decided to leave the box untouched. Maybe she'd feel better when she saw that he'd turned down the nephew's bribe, too.

On Friday when Doris Beasley came to pick up the dog for the weekend, she stopped again to update Duncan's parents on Astrid's progress. She brought the chocolates with her, the beribboned gold box clutched awkwardly against her trim, drab frame.

"You don't like candy?" she asked Duncan, proffering the lavish bait.

He shrugged.

"He's a chocoholic," Mom told her. "But shouldn't you take this box to Astrid?"

"That's the last thing she needs. If she's going to get around on her own, she has to keep off the pounds she's lost." It was clear that with Astrid's nephew back in New Jersey, Doris Beasley had taken over and was prepared to reign supreme in the Valentine household. "It's from the nephew. I thought Duncan might enjoy it."

"That's very thoughtful of you," Mom told her. "Maybe the staff at the rehab center would appreciate it."

Doris faced Duncan until he met her gaze. "You sure?" she asked.

He nodded. He managed to say, "Thanks, though." His symbolic statement of support seemed to have fallen flat.

But Doris had more to discuss than the box of candy. "Don't

go away, Duncan," she said as he started upstairs. "This involves you."

Instantly he thought of the shed and the lock with the splintered doorjamb. Or had Tracy blabbed about being in the house? He turned, leaned against the banister, and waited for her to go on.

But it was only about arrangements to bring Astrid home. If she continued to improve and could get in and out of bed on her own, then Doris would ease her into independence by staying there overnight for a while. The weekend was an ideal time to begin, because Doris could be there daytimes too. Astrid would have a walker to get herself to the bathroom. But even with Doris coming in after work, it would help a lot if Duncan continued to take care of the dog. Just for a while, Doris added. If no one objected.

Doris directed this last remark at Duncan's mother and father. Then everyone regarded Duncan expectantly.

Well? What did he think?

"I guess," he said. Then he blurted, "You know, Tracy Mattos might help. She's a girl."

"We know she's a girl," Mom said. "What are you getting at?"

"Well, Mrs. Valentine might be better off with a girl." He faltered. What was the matter with everyone? Couldn't they picture him walking in on Astrid Valentine while she was going to the bathroom?

"Tracy isn't used to the place like you are," Doris said. "She doesn't know the dog. You and Mo, you're getting along great. I was telling Astrid how crazy about you he is."

How did Doris know that? Duncan wondered. As far as he could tell, the dog was crazy about anyone who paid attention to him. If only Roz were home. She might speak up for him, remind Mom and Dad about that gross experience with Astrid Valentine.

"You don't have to commit yourself right now," Doris told him. "I'm sure there are lots of things you'd rather be doing than seeing to the dog every day. I wouldn't blame you if you decided to get back to your own life with your own friends. You just think it over and see whether you can spare another week or two. Just let me know, so we can get on with our plans."

He was sunk. He knew that. So did Doris Beasley. That was why she could afford to sound this understanding and generous.

After she was gone, the gold-wrapped box under her arm, he wondered how he had managed to lose everything, especially appreciation for holding out all week against the chocolate lure. No one had even noticed his symbolic gesture.

Late in the week an early March snowstorm nearly scuttled the target date for Astrid's homecoming. Thursday morning, while everyone in the Veerick house was still in bed, Duncan's friend Neil Gortler called. He had just heard the volunteer fire station whistle, the three short blasts and three long ones signaling no school.

This snow day was perfect. They would cross-country ski from the quarry through Ethan Cole's woods to just below Stark Bluff and then all the way to the river. A few kids besides Neil and Duncan had tried this before, but either the snow was too deep or the last leg on the plowed road with its traffic was too dangerous, prompting some parents to make the kids scale down their plans.

Not today, though. There was enough light for an earlier start. Duncan was up and out the door before his parents came downstairs. All he had to do was feed the dog, clear the snow away from the dog door, and shovel enough space outside for Mo to do his business.

Only after he'd slogged through the unplowed snow to get to the Valentine house did he realize he'd forgotten to bring along his family's snow shovel. Inside, he pushed past the scampering dog to get him out the kitchen door. Mo looked at the world outside and backed away. Duncan scooped him up and set him down on the porch. While he looked around for a shovel, the little dog ran to the door. Blocking and then holding him, Duncan scuffed and tramped to make a clearing. This time the dog made use of it. Still, Duncan wanted to shovel a path from the flap door for Mo, who might have to go out during the long day.

The shed was a good bet. Had he seen any rakes or shovels there? Duncan wasn't sure. He clambered over the gate and made his way to the shed door, which was easy enough to unlatch now but hard to open against the snow. Finally he managed to kick away enough of it to squeeze inside.

After the dazzling snow, the dim interior seemed cavernous. He felt his way along the wall, which was lined with things he couldn't identify but which he guessed were old farm implements. So far no shovel. On he went. He began to see shutters and ornate windows, some leaning, some stacked.

As he cut through to the opposite wall, his jacket sleeve brushed against the corner of a table, knocking off objects that thudded and clattered. He swung around to catch what he could, leaving the rest to be retrieved later. Deciding to get out of this place before all its movable parts trapped him, he made his way to the door with its narrow opening. It wasn't until he was outside that he realized he was still clutching something. A glass doorknob, cut like a gem. He headed for the gate.

Back in the yard, he called Mo. But the little dog refused to come to him. Or couldn't. Instead he huddled beside the kitchen door, looking pitiful and stubborn. To free both hands Duncan stuck the doorknob in his pocket and went to work clearing enough of an area beyond the dog door to allow Mo to get in and out on his own. Then, to show him it was possible now, Duncan grabbed the dog and shoved him through the door flap.

As soon as Duncan came into the kitchen, Mo scooted under a chair and eyed him with deep suspicion. Duncan found a bath towel and dragged the dog out to rub him dry. It didn't take long for Mo to revive. He even grabbed a corner of the towel and started to growl and shake it to death.

Not today, thought Duncan. Today he had big plans.

When he got home, Dad was shoveling the driveway. Mom came out, took the shovel, and said she'd finish if Dad wanted to get some breakfast. She looked meaningfully at Duncan, then glanced down the road toward the Valentine house.

Duncan said, "I didn't shovel the front there. I had to take care of the back door first. For the dog."

Mom nodded. "Okay," she said. "Have fun. I wouldn't mind having a snow day, too. But Rent-A-Tent needs your dad and I'm afraid Brixton Lumber can't do without me either."

Duncan said, "Want me to finish here?"

"No. You get breakfast. The plow's coming. We're almost out of here."

Inside, he decided to wait until Dad left the kitchen. So far neither parent had asked him about his plans for the day, and he didn't want to push his luck. He ran upstairs to change. It would be warm work cross-country skiing, especially the uphill miles. Water and a peanut butter sandwich would do. Maybe a chocolate bar if he could find one. He intended to travel light.

When he picked up his jacket again, he felt the doorknob in its pocket. He dug it out and and stuck it on the shelf with his garnets and arrowheads. He'd put it back in the shed some other time.

He waited until he heard Dad call upstairs to Roz. "You getting a ride with Denny? Roz? Regional's not canceled, you know. They're starting two hours late. You hear me?"

"Yes, I hear you," she answered from behind her closed door. "Yes, I'll go with Denny."

The front door closed, and a moment later Duncan heard the town plow scraping along the road. He waited until he heard the family car start up. Quick now, before Roz surfaced. In the kitchen he grabbed a few handfuls of granola, then ate a banana while he slathered peanut butter onto two slices of bread.

All set, he thought as he headed for his skis in the woodshed. He couldn't believe the gift of this day. Home free! Well, no, actually *away* from home free. Same thing, only better.

By the end of the day, as the boys approached Garnet Road, they were going single file because of the traffic, so conversation was impossible. Anyway, they were out of breath.

At the intersection they paused, leaning on their ski poles.

Neil said, "About now I wouldn't mind a cell phone in my pocket."

"You mean if we ever get coverage," Duncan responded.

"It'll happen," Neil said. "Soon as they agree on where to put the tower." He glanced at the sky, streaked orange and gray. "Maybe you should call my family when you get home. They always think the worst, like imagining a pack of coyotes bringing me down."

Duncan grinned. "I'll tell them you fought heroically."

"Your folks don't worry like that?" Neil asked.

Duncan shook his head. "Forget coyotes. It's drugs and sex that give them nightmares. My sister feeds their worst fears."

Neil laughed, and they parted.

It had been an exhilarating day, its high point the bobcat tracks they'd sighted and then followed until the rounded, four-toed prints zigzagged down the steep drop below Stark Bluff. But now Duncan was spent. When he came to the Valentine house and its unplowed driveway, he found himself hating this snow. He glanced up the road toward home. If you didn't know his own house was just ahead, you'd never guess there was a third dwelling on Garnet Road before it petered out, joining a rutted logging track in the upland woods.

After he let himself in, he fended off the little dog, then picked him up and carried him out to the yard. He waited just long enough to see Mo pee and begin to burrow through the snow, and then he went back inside. First he called Neil's mother, who sounded distracted and preoccupied with the younger kids shrieking too close to the phone. She thanked him for letting her know that Neil was on his way. Then he called home. The line was busy. Of course: Roz.

He still had to find a snow shovel. Or else borrow one? The Mattos farm would have plenty of shovels. He'd be surprised if they didn't have a snow blower, too. But they also had Tracy, and he was too tired to deal with any kind of Tracy invasion here.

Mo came barging through the dog flap and ran circles around Duncan before stopping to scratch at the cellar door. He wanted his big meal.

As Duncan scooped up kibble from the bag on the landing, it suddenly occurred to him to look downstairs for a shovel. First he put the food down for Mo. Then he switched on the light and went to look.

The cellar combined clutter with areas swept clean of all debris. It looked as though someone had gone at it full force and then abruptly stopped.

How long since Mr. Valentine had died? Duncan wasn't sure. A few years, anyway.

There was an ancient-looking workbench with various tools. There was a freestanding table saw devoid of sawdust. There was a closed cabinet as well as open shelves crammed with boxes and trays. Mr. Valentine must have been a pack rat. And everything lying idle since his death? It was hard to imagine Mrs. Valentine coming down here to sort through any of this.

Mo clattered down the stairs and leapt onto a pile of junk heaped in the corner behind the furnace. He began to claw at a clothes bag, then thrust his nose down between it and a scruffy suitcase.

"Come on," Duncan told him. "Out of here."

Mo scrambled down the far side of the pile and hurled himself at another door. His frantic scratching brought Duncan over to see what he was after.

The door opened into a stone-lined, windowless room. Duncan yanked on the string that dangled from a single overhead bulb, and its dim light revealed a row of large wooden boxes set on pallets. At first glance Duncan saw nothing inside the nearest ones but dirt. No, this was sand. Sticking his hand into it, he felt something small and hard. Recoiling, he drew back. Then curiosity took over. Even if it was a dead rat or something, it wasn't going to bite.

He found the lump again and then another and drew them out. At first glance under the lightbulb they seemed shapeless. But when he rubbed off the sand that stuck to them, he saw that they were shriveled roots. Beets? Maybe turnips. So this was a place for storing vegetables.

Meanwhile Mo had gone to explore. Duncan could hear him snuffling in the darkness. He wished he had a flashlight. Keeping his back to the wall so that he didn't block out the scant light from the bulb, he came to one more box or crate. This one seemed to be the one that attracted the dog. Duncan peered over and into it, but it was too dark to see anything. As far as he was concerned, he was finished here.

But Mo wasn't. He kept clawing at the crate as if determined to get at whatever was packed inside. Duncan groped around until his hand brushed up against a sack. Or was it a tarp? He pulled it up and draped it over the side, releasing a whiff of cold, musty air. Once again Duncan dug down inside the sand. Something was there, something big and limbed. Duncan's fingers began to discern a shape, and it chilled him to the bone. What had drawn Mo was some kind of lumpy figure wrapped in rags.

Duncan drew back. Then again, it wasn't going to bite. It had almost weirded him out simply because of the way it seemed to crouch under the sand. But it had to be some grungy, oversize doll, that was all.

Beside him, Mo pressed hard to get at the thing.

From what seemed miles off Duncan heard the phone ring. Quickly he shoved the tarp back, snatched up the dog, turned off the light, and ran out, slamming the door behind him.

When he picked up the phone, mid-ring, he was still clutching Mo.

"Duncan?" It was Mom. "What's the matter with you?"

"I was in the cellar," he said, trying to suppress his gasps. "Looking for a snow shovel."

"I was beginning to worry," she told him. "It's getting late."

"Yes. Sorry. Stop it," he said to the squirming dog in his face.

"What? Duncan? Come home now," she said.

"Yes," he answered, leaning down to set Mo on the floor.

Outside on the snowy granite step, he suddenly wondered if he had turned off the cellar light or even shut that door. Never mind; the kibble was out of reach and there wasn't much else Mo could get into down there. Duncan was absolutely sure he had closed the door to the root cellar.

Only after he had waded out to the road and was running home did he remember the skis and poles propped in the snow in front of the Valentine house. He kept going, though. He could get them tomorrow. All he could think of now was dinner and a hot shower.

Duncan blamed his lateness on the failed shovel search. Before he could finish telling his family about it, Roz broke in to say she bet Mrs. Valentine wouldn't appreciate him snooping around her house like that. Both parents defended him. Duncan wasn't a snoop, they said. He had been doing his best to make himself useful. After that exchange, Duncan decided to skip the doll thing.

"Just take our shovel over tomorrow," Dad said.

"Yes," Mom agreed. "And leave it there for now. Doris called and said the rehab people wanted to postpone the homecoming because of bad footing, but Astrid put up such a fuss that they gave in, providing all the snow is cleared off."

Full sun the next day helped with the after-school snow cleanup. Tracy caught on and brought over a shovel to help. When they finished the front entrance, they brought the shovels through the house and out the kitchen door to clear more yard space for Mo. He leapt and snapped at every scoop of snow that sailed past him. Duncan figured it was good exercise for him, but Tracy frowned on all that craziness.

"No manners," she observed.

Duncan swerved to avoid hitting Mo. "It's Mrs. Valentine's dog," was all he said.

"I don't know how she can stand it," Tracy retorted, obviously comparing the mop-with-a-mouth with the Mattos farm Border collie, a dog that knew its place.

Once or twice Duncan caught Tracy glancing toward the shed. Was this why she had come to help? Was she hoping for one last inspection before Astrid Valentine was home and the place would be off-limits? But Tracy didn't suggest going in there.

She rubbed off all the snow from her shovel before carrying it back into the house. Duncan leaned his shovel outside the kitchen door. He found her wiping away the few spots of melted snow they must have left when they came through from the front. She took her time with this cleanup, her eyes on all the features of the rearranged kitchen.

"Why not have the bed in the living room?" she asked.

He nodded toward the bathroom opposite the cellar door. "Closer," he said.

"Still … Where's the table?" Without waiting for an answer, she walked across the entry hall into the living room. "This doesn't make any sense," she said.

Duncan shrugged. He poured out Mo's kibble and set the dish down. "Thanks for helping," he told Tracy, taking her shovel to the front door.

Still in the living room, she called to him, "We could fix it. We could shove the sofa back and make room around the table so it doesn't block—"

"It's fixed," Duncan called back. "It's the way the nephew wanted it."

Finally she joined him. "Doris Beasley's staying with her this weekend?"

He nodded.

"We'll be over to visit. Mom will bring a casserole."

Duncan nodded again. He realized he'd better leave with Tracy to get her out. That meant he couldn't go downstairs with a flashlight for another look in the root cellar.

Well, it was none of his business anyway. Whatever that thing was, it had been there awhile, and it wasn't about to go anywhere.

The following afternoon when he and Tracy came walking up from the bus stop, Doris Beasley's car was parked out front.

"Looks like the Chicken Lady's home," Tracy said.

Duncan wasn't sure what to do. Was he supposed to stop in today? Or should he wait until Monday, when Doris had to be back at work? He hesitated, then decided to check, just in case Doris needed him.

At the door he pulled out his key and then used the door knocker instead. He rapped a couple of times before Doris came and opened the door.

"Don't you have a key?" she asked.

"Yes, but I didn't know if I should, you know, just walk in now."

"Oh, that's all right, Duncan. Yes, of course. When you let yourself in, just call out before you go into the kitchen in case she needs to cover up. Okay?"

He said, "She's home?"

"She is." Doris's exuberance made him tense up. "Why don't you come and say hi?" Her voice dropped. "Only for a minute. Coming home's a big deal, and she's wiped out."

He followed Doris into the kitchen, where a very changed Astrid Valentine lay propped, almost sitting, in the hospital bed. Her face looked thin, her arms flabby, and her gray hair had been cropped short. Mo lay snuggled beside her.

"Hello, Mrs. Valentine," he said awkwardly. Mo snailed around to look at him but otherwise stayed put.

Astrid Valentine said, "Astrid. I'm Astrid."

"Astrid," he said.

Doris said, "Duncan took wonderful care of Mo, and he'll be back Monday."

"Yes, I know," Astrid said. She spoke more slowly than he remembered, dragging her words a bit without actually slurring. "It was good of you. I'll find a way to thank you."

"That's all right," he told her, backing into the hall. Then he added, "I'll see you Monday."

Out on the road, he tried to remember what he had just said to her, how he had come across. Maybe he should have offered to run Mo around the yard or something. He couldn't imagine what it would be like on Monday when he had to face her alone.

At least he didn't have to do mornings anymore. After changing her mind three or four times over the weekend, Doris Beasley decided that his coming in would get Mo too excited, which was bound to disturb Astrid.

"Her sleep pattern's all messed up," Doris explained. "She doesn't want to take pills. And I don't blame her. See, she's already changed so much."

Dad said, "She should do what the doctor prescribes. Or discuss her reservations with him."

Doris shook her head. "I guess you don't know Astrid that well. She calls the shots."

Doris had come over to borrow a heating pad for Astrid and didn't seem in much of a hurry to get back. Dad said he was sorry they hadn't known about the heating pad before Natalie went shopping in Brixton—she could have picked one up. And Doris said it was too bad they didn't have cell phone service yet. Dad tried to walk Doris to the door before she launched into the cell tower issue. He had a hard time getting rid of her without being rude.

Before Duncan let himself into Astrid's house on Monday afternoon, he knocked on the door to alert her. But she wasn't in bed. She was leaning on her walker and scowling as she surveyed the altered living room.

"You know about this?" she demanded. "I can't even get through here."

Duncan said, "The … your nephew moved the table in there to make room for the bed next to the kitchen window."

"Eddie? He didn't say anything about this to me. Nor did Doris."

Duncan said, "I'll take Mo for a run out back."

"Wait," she said. "This is the first time I've come in here. Or tried to. It's impossible."

Duncan was at a loss. "After I give Mo—"

"Now! I can't stand like this all afternoon."

Mo gave up imploring Duncan to notice him and went to find a toy.

"Can you move the couch back to the wall?" she asked. "Where it belongs."

Duncan would be able to do that after shifting the table that blocked Astrid. "Maybe, if you move back," he said.

But when she tried stepping backward, the walker wouldn't budge. She swayed and grabbed for the back of a chair. Duncan jumped forward and caught it before it tipped over. Then, kneeling on the chair seat to hold it down, he reached for the walker and dragged it toward Astrid. Slowly, awkwardly, she transferred her grip from chair to walker. "God," she muttered, "how I hate this!"

When she was stable, Duncan said, "Can you turn around?"

"What an idiot I am," she said as she maneuvered herself and the walker. "I forget what I can't do anymore. Watch out, Mo, baby."

Duncan said, "I think the … Mr. Shoop was planning to put the table in the corner. That's why he pulled the couch out. I guess he never finished."

"All right," Astrid said from beside the desk. "We will. Table over to that end for now. Couch back where it was. Then we'll figure out where else to stick the table."

Duncan had to remove everything from the small table to maneuver the big one over it. Then after he got the couch off the rug, it wasn't hard to push it back and sideways.

"Leave it for now," Astrid told him. "I need to sit down. I'll figure out where else to fit things later." She paused to reach over to the desk, but her hand fell short. She said, "How about bringing the mail into the kitchen for me."

Once again the photograph of the woman with the microphone caught his eye. "Who is she?" he asked Astrid as he picked up the batch of mail.

"That?" Astrid uttered a sharp laugh like a bark. "Don't recognize her?"

Duncan said, "I'm not up on, well ..." He knew better than to say he didn't know the stars of olden times.

"Look again," Astrid told him. "That's me."

Speechless, he did look. From picture to person and back. Then once again. "When?" he asked.

"Oh," she said, "long ago when I made my living singing in clubs. Till Paul Valentine came along and swept me off my feet and out to the boonies. To this godforsaken place. I went from singing in New Jersey to raising chickens and hooking rugs in New England. What do you think of that?"

He couldn't reply.

She burst out laughing, this time with abandon. "You're a nice kid, Duncan. A really nice kid." Chortling, she shuffled across the hall to the kitchen and cautiously eased herself sideways onto the bed. "Go ahead. Take Mo," she told him.

Relieved, Duncan called Mo to the back door. He stayed outside long enough for the dog to wear himself out running circles in the cleared space or pouncing into deeper snow.

Back in the kitchen, Duncan found Astrid propped in the sitting position, not under the covers. She was still dressed in what he had assumed were pants but now looked like pajama bottoms, and she was still wearing the loose-fitting sweater on top. Beside her on the wheeled bed table was an array of books and snacks along with the telephone and a pitcher and mug.

"How's my boy?" she demanded, greeting Mo, who scrambled to climb into the bed. She reached down for him despite Duncan's warning that the dog was wet.

When Duncan went for the dog food behind the cellar door, he saw two gift baskets with fruit and nuts and preserves there. He hoisted one up and asked Astrid if she wanted anything.

"Look at that one," she said, pointing to a third gift basket next to a vase full of flowers on the Hoosier cabinet. "Help yourself. It'll go bad before I get through even one basket. No, I mean it, Duncan," she insisted as he shook his head. "It's really good of everyone, but even I have my limits."

Mo watched from the bed as Duncan set down the dish of kibble. The dog pricked up his ears, interested, but not enough to abandon his perch on the bed.

Astrid said, "Before you go, could you heat up the kettle? And you'll find the ginger tea up there above the flour bin. And I need the trash basket closer."

He waited for the requests to wind down. Even then it was hard to walk out on her.

The following afternoon Astrid was on her bed and either sleepy or depressed. Duncan attended to Mo and then quietly left.

Wednesday was different. It was a half day for the middle school kids. When he showed up early, he found Astrid at her desk in the living room sorting through packets of letters and photographs.

"Look at this!" she said as he came into the hall.

Stepping around the twirling dog, he glanced over to peer at the snapshot of a soldier with his arm around a girl. She didn't look like the woman in the framed picture. "That's Paul," she said. "And that's his first wife before they were married."

Paul her husband? Duncan said, "Oh. When was that?"

"Before me," she said. "Korea. Probably sometime after the war." She swiveled in the chair, using the walker to brace herself. "This is what people do when they get old," she told him. "They look back. Sometimes at people they never knew."

Finding it impossible to respond to this, he switched subjects. "Where was that picture of you taken?" he asked.

She glanced at the image of her former self and shook her head. "You know, I'm not sure. I sang in clubs all over New Jersey and in the Poconos. It was a great life. I met all kinds of people, all types. For a while my boyfriends were drummers." She sighed.

"Which is odd, because it was the brass I favored."

Duncan said, "I'm learning to play trumpet."

"No kidding? You're my man, then!"

"I'm not very good yet," he added. "Right now I'm learning from a method book." He had missed lessons and band practice since his commitment to Mo began, but he couldn't come out and say that.

"You do jazz?" she asked.

He shook his head.

"You like it?"

"I guess so," he answered. "Mostly we do marching stuff."

"I'll put on some good pieces for you to hear. Paul was taping our favorites before he died. Lately I guess I've just stopped listening. Except I play loud, hot music during electric storms to drown out the thunder. I do that for Mo here. There's a cassette player somewhere. Probably upstairs. Doris will find it."

"Come on, Mo," Duncan said, heading for the kitchen and the back door. He didn't want to hurt Astrid's feelings, but she sounded as though she would go on talking nonstop if he didn't break away.

He glanced over the yard fence at the shed door. Another look inside would relieve the boredom of being outside with Mo. Besides, he still hadn't picked up the things that had fallen. Only now that Astrid was home, he was uneasy about going in without permission.

Before he left, he asked Astrid whether it was all right to feed Mo this early. She answered from the living room that there was no problem. "Take some fruit," she said.

So he helped himself to a banana and a pear, and then he said goodbye and left.

That night he asked his parents if someone else ought to take over with Astrid, since she seemed so lonely. Someone who could talk with her. They said they had no idea who could keep her company that way. Wanda Mattos might visit, but she was overwhelmed with farm work. Besides, after Mace shot up the Valentine sign, relations between the two families never did fully mend. Anyway, Duncan was used to the dog and the dog was used to him.

The best he could hope for the next day was that he would find Astrid in bed and turned off. But once again she was in the living room, and this time she was stuck.

"Trapped," was the way she put it. "I need some of this crap out of here, or I'll never get around."

At least today she was too irritated to share. After he shifted furniture again and rolled up the rug and set two chairs on the couch, he dealt with Mo and left without further conversation.

In school on Friday Neil asked him over that afternoon. But there was no way to get home from Neil's house in time to take care of the dog, so Duncan had to say no.

"You know what this was called in colonial times?" Neil said.

Duncan shook his head.

"Indentured servitude," Neil told him. "When people worked for nothing to pay off their passage, or something like that."

Duncan said, "Only with me there's nothing to pay off. It's all about being a good neighbor."

"Bummer," said Neil. "Maybe Saturday we can go to Brixton and do the rock wall."

"If we can get there," Duncan answered. "I think my dad's doing tent setups all weekend. With outdoor events starting up again, he takes every tent rental he can get."

"Let's work on it," Neil said. "I'll reserve us an hour."

When Duncan walked up the road from the bus there was a car parked in front of Astrid's house. A visitor meant he could get in and out in no time. He knocked extra loud before letting himself in and found Astrid sitting on the bed and her guest on a kitchen chair with a folder and papers on his knee. Even dressed in jeans and a sweatshirt, the man looked like someone who cared about neatness. Duncan noticed especially the clean, white hands.

"Do you two know each other?" Astrid asked.

Duncan started to shake his head, but the man shifted the folder, leaned forward, and said, "Duncan? I met your father. Call me Eddie."

The nephew with a different car. Duncan nodded. He tried to make his way to the back door, but Eddie Shoop had more to say.

"You clear off all the snow? That made a big difference here."

Duncan said, "Tracy Mattos helped."

"Who's he?" asked Eddie Shoop.

"She. She lives across the road, at the farm. She brought another shovel." He turned to Astrid. "I never did find yours. I've still got ours over here."

Eddie Shoop said, "Tracy who?" To Astrid he added, "Like I said, if you'd keep track of all these good people, we'd be sure they were thanked properly. Right?"

Astrid said, "Sure, Eddie. Right. That's Tracy Mattos. Her uncle's the nut case who objected to Paul painting a peace symbol on our sign. Objected with bullets. Mace was wounded in Vietnam. Wounded in more ways than one. His wife left him, so he lives with his brother Bud and their old man and of course

Wanda and the one girl still at home. Mace can drink himself out cold. Wanda brought over a stew. Don't worry, Eddie, I was properly grateful. And there's more damn fruit and stuff on the cellar landing."

"Don't talk that way," he told her. "I'm trying to set things up here so that you can manage on your own, but you'll need a hand from time to time, and no one's going to feel obliged to help you if they're not appreciated."

"Eddie," Astrid said, "the last thing I need is life lessons from you. Except," she added, "when it comes to the insurance upgrade and that kind of thing."

"Okay," Eddie responded. "I'm just trying to get things going. It's hard to do it all from a distance. Go ahead with Mo," he said, dismissing Duncan. "This is just a minor family squabble."

"Don't worry about Duncan," Astrid declared. "He's my friend. He'll even eat my fruit." She grinned at Duncan, waving him out.

When Duncan came back in, Astrid and Eddie were embroiled in an argument about taxes.

"As far as I can tell," Eddie ranted, "you're three years behind on your property tax, and I can't find any record of last year's income tax."

"No income, no tax," Astrid declared.

"What do you live on? Where's the money come from?"

Astrid said, "When I'm short, I sell something. Call up one of the dealers Paul did business with. They come. Someone always pays."

It was clear that neither of them had noticed Duncan's return.

"Astrid," Eddie told her, "they could be robbing you blind, for all you know. Some of that stuff Paul acquired is worth a bundle."

Astrid chuckled. "You don't know the half of it."

Duncan kicked the dog door. As it flapped in and out, he stomped over to get the kibble. Eddie and Astrid fell silent for a moment.

Then Eddie asked, not impatiently, "All set?"

"Almost," Duncan replied, wondering why Eddie couldn't feed Mo as long as he was here. Duncan took the water bowl to the sink. If only he could be finished here, finished for good.

Astrid said, "Eddie, you're a good boy to come and help your old aunt."

Boy? thought Duncan. He snatched a quick glance at Eddie Shoop, who looked no younger than Dad.

"Trouble is, you worry too much," Astrid continued. "Doesn't he?" she demanded, suddenly dragging Duncan into the middle of the discussion.

"I don't know," he mumbled, rinsing out the bowl for the second time. He wanted to leave, but he wasn't sure whether Astrid had included him now to keep him here.

"So look at it this way," Eddie said, shoving his chair back and slamming the folder down on his closed laptop. "I won't be visiting this often now that you're on your feet, so I'm going to have to do some of your business online. We'll need a website to move things along."

"What things?" Astrid demanded. "Set up what?"

"It's a way to connect with customers." He paused.

Duncan decided to make a break for it. Only now there wasn't enough room behind Eddie.

"To begin with," Eddie resumed, "you need some ready cash. As far as I can make out, you've got three different accounts, all of them practically empty. We can straighten that out, but first I'll deposit some money in at least one you can write checks on."

Astrid grunted. "What money? Where from?"

"For starters, from me. Just to keep you solvent, Astrid. You can pay me back after the next sale."

Duncan sidled closer. "Excuse me," he murmured, squeezing past.

"Wait up," Eddie told him. "I just had an idea. Before we can set prices, we ought to know exacly what's here. We need an inventory for the insurance anyway. Duncan, could you help out if I organize it for you? I'll list the categories. All you have to do is count."

"Tracy!" Duncan blurted. Why him again? Hadn't he done enough for them? "Tracy would be good at that. She loves—" He stopped short.

"Loves what?" prompted Eddie.

"Well, different stuff," Duncan said, scrambling to come up with something plausible. "She loves a change from the farm. She came over here and helped me shovel snow." Duncan guessed he was on solid ground now. In spite of his blunder, he hadn't told on her.

Astrid said, "We can think about it. Let Duncan go now, Eddie. He's had enough of us."

Duncan hesitated. Was he supposed to say of course not, he'd be glad to stay and talk? No way, he thought. He wouldn't be glad. He eased himself out of the kitchen and through the front door.

It wasn't until he was outside that it occurred to him that he should have mentioned payment. If there was any chance of getting Tracy over here to count doorknobs, Astrid and Eddie needed to understand that she wouldn't work for nothing. Maybe if they knew that, they wouldn't even consider asking her. Or maybe Eddie, who was about to put some money in Astrid's account, would be prepared to pay for her time and effort. He might even take the next obvious step and pay Duncan as well.

"You missed a whole soap opera episode," Roz said as Duncan came in with Dad. It was Saturday evening, and she was waiting for Denny to pick her up.

"Don't exaggerate," Mom said to her. "And stop being mean about Doris."

Dad said, "Sorry we're so late, Nat. Everything took longer than I expected. Not the boys. They were at the lot ahead of me."

"That was fine with us," Duncan said. The full day in Brixton had been great, with two rock-climbing sessions. He and Neil had been ready to wind down when they went to the tent office to wait for Duncan's father, where they'd made a considerable dent in its welcome box of nearly day-old doughnuts.

He followed Roz into the living room. "What's going on with Doris?" he asked.

Roz peered out the window into the darkness. "Everyone's late tonight," she muttered.

Duncan supposed "everyone" meant Denny.

"What's going on?" he asked again.

Kneeling on the couch and facing the window, she said dismissively, "You know. Jealousy. Hurt feelings." She turned to him. "They act like middle schoolers."

"We middle schoolers don't act like anything," he protested. "Anyway, who's 'they'?"

"They. The Valentine people. Doris Beasley practically in tears. No one warned her that the nephew was back. So she goes there with the shopping bags and cooked food, ready to do the wash and all that, and the nephew tells her to get lost. He's trying to come between her and Astrid, she says. Then she leaves her roast chicken with Mom so the nephew won't get any. You're supposed to take it over Monday." Headlights shone outside the window. "Finally!" she exclaimed. "I'm going," she yelled into the kitchen.

All Duncan could think as he went in to supper was how lucky he was to have been away all day, far from those people and their drama.

But his luck had just run out. His mother informed him that Eddie Shoop had called to ask him to come over Sunday afternoon to go over some matters they'd already discussed.

"You know what he means?" Mom asked.

Duncan shrugged. "Maybe. I'm not going."

"Wait a minute," Dad said to him. "You had all of today for yourself. Don't you think you ought to at least give the guy a chance? Hear what he has to say?"

"No! I'm tired of being there every day. You don't know what it's like."

"Aren't you overreacting?" Dad asked. "Tell you what—I'll go with you."

Duncan couldn't look at his father. How could Dad be so clueless? "If you're there, it'll be different."

"Exactly. I'll be there to back you up."

Duncan gave up. There was nothing more to say.

But by Sunday noon Dad had two emergency calls. That was the trouble with March setups. Between the frozen ground and high winds, weekend tent problems were always cropping up. "Sorry to bail on you," he told Duncan.

Mom offered to go over with Duncan instead. She had made a lasagna to bring to Astrid, since Doris didn't want the roast chicken there till the nephew was gone.

They walked down to the Valentine house, which looked as though a tornado had swept through it. Everything seemed to have blown into the kitchen and piled up there. Even on the bed. Astrid reclined there surrounded by bowls and a few carved bones and lots of stone people and weathervane crests and lanterns and scrimshaw tusks. Mo yelped from the yard. The dog door had been blocked to keep him out.

Duncan's mother stood at the edge of the pileup, speechless, clasping the lasagna.

"Hey, there!" Eddie crowed. "Duncan! Good man. And … ?"

"My mother," he said.

"Natalie Veerick," she said.

"Glad to meet you. Sorry about all this. I'm trying to get things set up for Astrid."

Mom said, "How are you doing, Astrid? I hope there's room in the fridge for this. There's enough to last for several meals."

"Thanks, Natalie. Good of you," Astrid said. "Eddie will deal with it."

Stepping over a birdbath, Eddie took the lasagna pan. "Smells wonderful," he declared.

Mom said, "I hope you're able to find the oven by dinnertime."

For a moment they all surveyed the chaos in the kitchen.

Then Eddie said, "Maybe Duncan told you about my project. To inventory, then get everything appraised." He turned to his aunt. "I still can't believe you never insured any of this."

Astrid said, "Why should I? What can happen to it? It's worth whatever someone will pay for it."

"Look at that," Eddie told her, pointing to a stone walrus. "Eskimo art is always in demand. It could be worth thousands."

"Not for sale," Astrid told him. "When I'm dead you can do what you want with it."

Mom said, "How did you get it? And all those other things?"

"One of Paul's cleanouts. You'd be surprised what people don't bother with. They just call up the salvage man, that's Paul, and tell him to clear the premises. There's more Eskimo stuff around here. Some beautiful, some ugly. Dealers go for them. Artifacts. Doesn't matter what they look like."

"Well," Mom said to Astrid, "I guess this isn't the best time for a visit." She turned to Eddie. "How long are you staying?"

"Oh, I'm off home tomorrow," he told her. "I'd leave today, but I want to get to the bank in Brixton."

Duncan's mother told him she worked in Brixton at the lumber company.

"And your husband? He works in Brixton, too, doesn't he?"

Duncan's mother nodded. "He manages Rent-A-Tent."

"Well, who knows? Maybe I'll be able to talk Astrid into holding an auction here and we'll need a big tent for it."

"In a pig's eye," Astrid muttered.

Duncan's mother said, "Well, enjoy the lasagna, and I'll be over again, Astrid."

Duncan thought he was home free, but Eddie said, "Wait, Duncan. I made a list for the shed count. The sooner you get started there, the better."

"Waste of his time," Astrid remarked. "He should be practicing the trumpet."

"Hold on," Eddie objected. "I'm going to pay him for his time. All he has to do is keep track of it. And, Astrid, the lock isn't even attached to the shed. Anyone could go in there. Right, Duncan?"

Duncan said, "Um, I guess so. But why would they?"

"Believe me, there's some that might. A lot of what looks like junk, it's what some people are crazy for. That shed is like a warehouse full of one-of-a-kind antique fixtures. And the lock's hanging loose. Anyone can walk in. Next time I come I'll bring a new one, since I can't talk Astrid into installing an alarm system."

"Can I get Tracy to help?" Duncan blurted.

Mom said, "We can replace the lock if you like."

"Thanks, but there's nothing to attach it to but rotted wood. Astrid's lucky to have neighbors like you. I wish she wasn't so far out of town, but I know this was Paul's family home. I don't blame her for feeling sentimental."

"Bull!" Astrid declared. "I'm settled, that's all. I lie here and look across the valley. I have a view of coated round hay bales and the non-milking Mattos cows on the slope. What more could I ask for except an uncluttered pathway to my bathroom?"

Eddie laughed. "All you have to do is ask, and I'll make room."

Duncan's mother, trying to get to the front door, said, "Our house has been in the family for generations, too. I know how Astrid feels. Our kids wish we'd move into Brixton, and I have to admit we're sometimes tempted to. But ..." She opened the door.

Walking home, Duncan's mother kept shaking her head. "If you ask me," she remarked, "Doris is well out of it this weekend."

Me too, thought Duncan. He couldn't imagine what the place would be like when he stopped by on Monday afternoon.

On Monday Astrid seemed on edge and distracted.
She barely noticed the chicken Duncan stuck in her refrigerator. Twice she asked him to go upstairs to look for her box of tapes. Both times she bellowed at him to come down before he had a chance to follow through.

"I can't find what I need," she said. "Every damn thing's been moved." Standing in the hall, she cast her eyes over what she could see of the living room. She shifted the walker sideways, then declared, "If I can't do anything, I might as well get off my feet." With that, she shuffled around to the kitchen, where in record time she pulled and slid and then heaved herself onto the bed. Anger seemed to have energized her.

"Duncan," she said, "see if you can find my album in there. I don't know where Eddie put it."

A CD album? A DVD? It had to be something connected with the tapes that were supposed to be upstairs. As he lifted and replaced things and squeezed farther back, he could tell that Eddie had made a stab at putting things in order. But there was a lot that remained unshelved, some pieces stacked in precarious balance, others just shoved together.

After he came up empty, Astrid sighed and closed her eyes.

"You want me to keep looking for the tapes?" he asked her.

She shook her head. "Doris will find them."

But Doris wasn't coming until next weekend. He said, "I'll take Mo out now."

Astrid didn't reply. Then, after he called Mo to the back door, she spoke again. "It's nasty here. I didn't get clean sheets. Or anything else clean." Since she didn't seem to be aiming these remarks at him, he let himself and Mo out into the yard.

Although much of the snow was gone, there were stretches of it along the shed and under the porch eaves where the sun didn't reach. He made snowballs and threw them for the dog to pounce on. He dreaded going back in and being sent on another hopeless search.

After Mo's playtime, Duncan gave him his food, which he gulped down so fast he choked on some of it. Duncan wondered when he'd last been fed. He glanced at Astrid to see if she'd noticed. She seemed unaware of Mo's state, so Duncan gave him an extra scoop of kibble.

That was all, then. He could leave now.

Still, it wasn't all that easy to walk out of the house. Astrid, the control switch in her hand, lowered the head of the bed. She looked so awkward there, her blue slacks hiked up, her thick ankles bare.

Then he was out of the house and breathing in the early spring air.

At home he started a video game. He wasn't really into it, though. Neil was an avid gamer, so once in a while Duncan made a stab at playing. But it was more fun when they did it together.

Maybe there was something on the tube. Roz used to claim she could distinguish one sitcom or soap character from another. As far as he could tell, they were either dupes or schemers, almost all of them accident-prone. What world did they come from? He thought of Tracy in her living room, probably glued to the screen. He tried to guess which channel she'd be watching, then gave it up. Now, while he was still alone, was his one chance to practice on the trumpet Mr. Simon let him use. Digging out his method book along with the trumpet, he went to work. As always, the tinny notes he produced fell far short of what he expected when he heard the music inside his head. Still, he kept at it until the front door slammed and Roz came in.

"Getting there," she said. "You might make it."

Sometimes she could be so nice. He said, "Astrid Valentine says she used to sing in clubs."

"Who's she kidding?" Roz said. "You believe her?"

"I don't know. There's this hot picture. From that time."

"Huh," said Roz noncommittally.

Duncan let the subject drop. He didn't even know why he'd mentioned it.

It wasn't until Thursday that Astrid handed Duncan the lined pad that Eddie had left for him. There was a note on it with an example, four parallel marks, a fifth mark slashed across them. Eddie had divided the shed stuff into general categories like lighting, windows and shutters, hardware for doors, and plumbing fixtures, and he had then listed subgroups. He hoped all of these would be inventoried by the time he returned in a couple of weeks. Duncan should keep track of the time he spent counting.

"Sorry I didn't give this to you before," Astrid said. "It slipped my mind until I found it today with some other things I was looking for. See?" She held up a photograph album.

It came to him that this must be the album she'd had in mind the other day.

"I've been doing some sorting." She sounded stronger and calmer. "Eddie has a point about keeping track of what's here. Want to see some of these?"

When she held the album open invitingly, Duncan felt obliged to look. There were pictures of a man in uniform. Obviously Paul. On the facing page there were shots of Paul and Astrid together.

Looking at the young Astrid while the old Astrid hovered beside him was surreal. It was hard to believe that the sleek, elegant woman tipping her chair back, her legs upraised, feet resting on a railing, a cigarette dangling from one hand, could have become this pasty creature in baggy pajama bottoms and drooping sweater. Yet there were the same eyebrows and bold forehead. He wasn't sure about the eyes, though, and he wondered about the voice, throaty now, almost gravelly. Could it have been sexy once?

Pleading homework and tomorrow's math test, Duncan pulled away from her to take care of the dog. He didn't even consider starting in the shed. It would take days to get all the stuff counted. Unless he had help.

Friday afternoon he told Tracy about the project and invited her to join him sometime over the weekend.

"How much is he paying?" she asked.

When Duncan told her that the amount hadn't been mentioned, she said, "I don't know. Maybe." Then she asked, "Does he know about me, the nephew?"

Duncan said, "I asked. He didn't say no."

"And they're getting it done for a sale?"

"Maybe. Probably. Anyway, Astrid Valentine lives on what she sells."

Tracy said, "Mom brought her soup the other day and says the place is a mess. There's food that's gone bad and good food that the Chicken Lady hasn't touched."

Without mentioning Eddie Shoop's power grab last weekend, Duncan told Tracy he thought Doris Beasley would probably take care of all that.

"Okay," Tracy said. "I guess I'll come. It could be interesting."

Maybe she knew more than she let on about the tension between the nephew and Doris. If Roz heard it as soap opera, that could be Tracy's take, too. Whatever turned her on, thought

Duncan. All that mattered to him was that he wouldn't be alone in that dreary shed counting row upon boring row of doorknobs.

When they met on the road Saturday morning, Tracy wanted to go through the house to get to the shed in back. Duncan reminded her that the yard gate didn't work and it would be harder to get over the fence from bare ground. Besides, Astrid might not be up yet or else getting a bath, now that Doris was there to help her.

So they walked past the rusty stoves and a few old sinks almost hidden in brush and debris. Farther along, the chicken house leaned against rotting posts that had once led to the weed-clogged coop. Duncan and Tracy had to double back for a bit to avoid last year's barbed blackberry canes and the tangled bittersweet that had taken over that end of the driveway. It wasn't until they were inside the shed that Duncan remembered the pad. Telling Tracy he'd be right back, he vaulted over the fence, knocked, and then opened the kitchen door and called inside.

Mo came flying at him.

"Hello?" he called, stepping around a heap of sheets and towels.

"In here," Astrid shouted from the living room.

"I just came for the pad and pencils," he said, retrieving them from the Hoosier cabinet.

Doris came into the kitchen. "Good," she said. "Take the dog with you."

"I can't. I mean, not outside the yard. We're working in the shed."

"Lord," she said with a groan. "Have you seen the mess he left?"

Duncan nodded. "It was worse before."

"Poor Astrid. She thinks everything's getting away from her.

Nothing's where it should be. It's not good for her to get this riled. I'm sure it's not."

"Still," Duncan said, "she does have better days."

"You think?" Doris asked.

Duncan nodded. What did he know about Astrid's condition? Still, seeing her every day, he could tell that she had her ups as well as her downs. "Yes. She'll probably feel a lot better now that you're here."

"Doris!" Astrid shouted from the living room. "You coming? Don't leave me stranded here."

Doris turned and hurried back to her. Duncan left quickly. Of course Mo banged through the dog door and ran with him to the fence.

"Stay," Duncan told him, a futile command. The dog yipped and hurled himself at the gate as Duncan tossed the pad and pencils to the other side and then followed them over.

"That took a while," Tracy remarked from the far end of the shed.

"Yes," Duncan agreed. "Another reason not to go through the house."

"Where do we start?" Tracy asked. "How about colored windows first? They're amazing."

So they began the count, taking turns sorting and tabulating. The dust they stirred up made their eyes tear, and they sneezed a lot.

Tracy liked handling things and matching separate parts. "What do you suppose this is for?" she kept asking. Or she would pause to examine an old faucet and wonder why anyone would want it instead of a new one.

On they went, the counting tedious and seemingly endless.

When they finally called it quits, they weren't even halfway through.

Tracy looked over the tabulations. "Let's add up what we've got so far." She began to count out loud by fives. "Four hundred and twenty-three hinges!" she exclaimed. "A lot of nothing."

They left the way they had come, skirting the house. Even Tracy had had enough.

The moment Duncan walked into the house his mother took one look at him and gasped. "Don't take another step," she ordered. "Just strip down."

"Here?" He looked at the grime coating his jeans, his jacket and shirt.

"Here," she answered. "Then shower."

He raced naked upstairs to the bathroom. The water ran gray off his head and body. Well, what did everybody expect? First they were after him to help Astrid, and then they treated him as though he were toxic. So let them get him a hazmat suit. Put up or shut up.

By the time he was cleaned up and dressed, his indignation had fizzled. All he said when he came downstairs was that one day a weekend in the shed was enough. No one disagreed.

Monday morning Tracy informed him that she was in no hurry to finish the counting. "I hope you haven't got a deadline, but, well, all that stuff I inhaled, it's worse than hay dust. I can deal with the barn."

Duncan let her off the hook. He told her he hadn't realized how bad it would be. He was thinking of skipping next weekend himself.

When he stopped at the Valentine house that afternoon, one glance into the living room was all it took to see that the place was transformed. So was Astrid, who couldn't wait to show him what Doris had found.

"She must've worked straight through the night," Duncan said.

"She stayed over, got up early Sunday morning, and just kept going all day. She found these tapes up in the spare room." Astrid pointed to a cardboard carton full of audio cassettes. "Treasures!" she exclaimed.

After he'd given Mo a good race around the back yard, he went straight to the cellar landing for dog food. Astrid was still in the living room. Could he make it out the front door without being stopped? He thought about retreating out the back way. But Astrid's voice brought him up short. "In here," she commanded. "Duncan?"

She was sitting at her desk with a flat box in front of her that turned out to be an ancient tape player. "Listen to this," she told him. She started the player.

How long before he could get away? He was standing in the front hall, one eye on the door while trying to look attentive, appreciative. At first what he noticed was that the sound system was awful. No way to hear music. Still, if it was all she had, he supposed it was better than nothing. He listened. It was some kind of jazz combo. There was a trumpet. There was ... a trumpet wrapping notes around itself and then flinging them straight through the roof. When the set ended, there was applause, suddenly cut off.

"A live performance," he said.

"Live then," Astrid said. "Dead now. You know who it is?"

He shook his head.

"Louis Armstrong. Ever heard of him? Of Satchmo?"

"I know who he is. I mean, I thought he was a singer."

"That too. With a gravelly voice. When Mo was a puppy he growled when he heard it. And howled when the notes hit high. That's how he got his name. Mo for Satchmo. You want to hear more?" she asked.

He went to the couch and sat down. She flipped out the cassette, inserted another. This was a cleaner recording. Jazz again, but different. Trumpet, too. He didn't speak. Neither did she until the end of the piece.

Then she said, "That's Wynton Marsalis."

He didn't tell her that he'd never heard of Wynton Marsalis. He just nodded. Then he said, "I really don't know anything about jazz." He started to get up.

Out came that tape, and in went another. This was something else. Not a trumpet. Well, not any trumpet sound Duncan recognized. He scowled in puzzlement. The clear, sweet notes, the intricate runs—they were unlike anything he had ever heard. He shook his head.

"Telemann," she said.

"A trumpet?" he asked.

She nodded. "Different kind. Older model."

"So this guy Telemann is older than Louis Armstrong?"

She said, "Telemann's the composer. It's still Wynton Marsalis."

"Oh." Too many names coming at him all at once. Again he rose to his feet. "I'd better get going. I do my trumpet practice before anyone else comes home. I don't sound anything like those guys," he added.

"No one does," she answered with a smile. "A lot of people wish they did, though."

On his way to the door he paused. He said, "I just want to be good enough to play in the high school band when I get there."

"Sensible goal. Realistic. Still, it doesn't mean you can't enjoy the great trumpeters now and again. We'll listen to more some other time."

"Cool," he said.

Walking home, his head full of that amazing music, he thought, well, it was a tradeoff. He'd definitely go back to work in the shed next Saturday.

The music, listening together, changed every-
thing. The jazz was riveting. Duncan wasn't sure what to make of
the classical stuff, although that other trumpet, the one Wynton
Marsalis sometimes used, made the sweetest sound. Baroque.
He learned that word from Astrid. Of course he asked why a
famous musician would use a broke trumpet. She explained
that a baroque trumpet was older, a classical instrument. It
turned out that there were various kinds of trumpets, like Louis
Armstrong's cornet.

When Astrid talked about all of this, she skipped the adult-to-
kid tone he was used to. Even when he exposed his ignorance, she
just dealt with him as a fellow human being. And then she found
a tape with someone named Roger Voisin playing another not-
broken trumpet. The quality of the recording was crummy, but
the music was something else.

On Saturday Duncan continued the inventory on his own, but
without Tracy it was slow going. Maybe if she joined him next
weekend they could finish the job and get paid.

Astrid seemed unaware of what he was up to in the shed. These
days she was either fumbling with her cassettes or listening to
them, eyes closed.

One day the following week she told him she'd been putting
off asking him for a favor. "I get distracted," she said. "That's

what the old music does to me." Then she informed him that her first husband had played the trumpet.

Duncan hadn't known about a first husband. After a moment he asked, "Was he good?"

"Very good. In all ways." Astrid laughed. "Then he got himself killed. Of course you build people up when they're gone. All I know is we made good music together."

Duncan let this sink in. "What happened to his trumpet?" he asked.

"Oh, I kept it awhile. Even after Paul and I were married. Then we needed money, and I let Paul sell it. He could find a buyer for almost anything. Even for those ghastly Peruvian mummies he picked up. At first he didn't know it was illegal to have them. But they were hot, and he unloaded one after another and never got into trouble."

Duncan, astonished, asked, "Mummies like from Egypt?"

"Sort of," Astrid told him. "Only the ones from Peru aren't packed in cases. They're folded up. Actually, they were kind of hideous, but they had gorgeous wrappings."

"Where did they come from?" he asked, adding quickly, "I know, Peru. But where did your husband get them?"

"One of those estates that had to be dismantled by the absent heirs. They hired Paul to finish the job. He picked up his best salvage fixtures from those removals. Only this time he comes home with a truck full of mummies."

"What did he do with them?"

"Oh, they hung around for a while. I don't know how many. He lined them up against the shed wall, freaked out some customers, intrigued others. First time, I think Paul practically gave one away. Then along comes a guy who makes a sizable offer on a couple. Then the guy came back for more. Paul jacked the price up. Someone else came. Up and up. Good big money, those mummies. But I was glad to be rid of them."

"They're all gone?" Duncan asked. Could the thing he'd seen in the root cellar be a mummy? Had he actually touched it? He couldn't remember. Well, yes, he had dug sand away from it. Was that hideous thing he'd taken for a doll a dead person?

"They'd better be. I wouldn't want to be caught with one these days. It could land you in a heap of trouble."

"Why? What kind of trouble?" If he told her what he'd seen, he'd be admitting that he'd gone snooping.

Astrid shrugged. "A big fine, I suppose. I think it's like owning wild animals. Used to be all right, but now you can't unless you're authorized by some agency. Anyway, people used to get away with importing things like mummies. No more."

It was now or never. If he didn't mention what he'd glimpsed, how could he speak of it later? He said, "Before you came home I went looking for a snow shovel. I went downstairs. I saw something … something … I didn't know what it was. I still don't. It was something like an enormous doll."

"Duncan! Really? Why didn't you tell me?"

"Well, I am now. I forgot about it until you mentioned those mummies. It might not be one."

"Well, go down and look. Take a good flashlight."

"What if I can't tell what it is even with a flashlight? Maybe you should wait for Eddie."

"No. Definitely not Eddie. Aren't you curious about it?"

"I was. I guess I am." But if it was in bad shape and valuable as well as illegal, he didn't feel like wading in over his head. Maybe with Tracy? They could explore together. He said, "When

I have more time. Saturday, when Tracy and I finish up in the shed. Then we can check out the root cellar."

That seemed to satisfy Astrid, who was beginning to look toward the kitchen. When she tired, she would stagger to her feet, lean heavily on the walker, and shuffle back to bed while she still had the strength to get herself there.

"Duncan," she said as he moved away from her, "that favor I mentioned. Will you do it for me?"

He paused, awaiting orders.

"The last time I sang in public was in Chiswick in the First Parish Church. I guess you can call it public. It was at Paul's funeral. I sang one of our favorites, 'When the Saints Go Marching In.' "

Duncan nodded. He had no idea what she was leading up to. Maybe she was distracted again and had forgotten about the favor.

"It's a great song for a sendoff," Astrid said. "So what I'd like," she told him, "is for you to learn it on your trumpet. Then when I die, you play it for me. Will you?"

Taken by surprise, at first all he could manage was an awkward nod. "I'll try," he said, thinking he'd have to ask Mr. Simon to find him the music. "I guess I have plenty of time to learn it."

"You never know," she replied cheerfully. "Anyway, now that I've asked you, it's finally off my mind."

The next time Duncan saw Astrid, Monday after- noon, she was in bed. She just grunted at him as he came through the kitchen. So he hurried outside and threw sticks for Mo until the little dog flopped down on his belly.

Back inside, Duncan attended to the food and water. Astrid ignored him, and he left quickly.

The following days were much the same. Astrid hardly stirred. She didn't even greet Mo when he came to her.

On Thursday Duncan paused on his way to the door. "Anything you want?" he asked.

She growled something he didn't understand.

"What?"

"Oh, just go," she told him. "There's nothing you can do about it."

"About what?" As soon as he spoke, he realized he should have taken her response for a no and left.

But now she rolled onto her side and propped herself up on one elbow. "It looks like Eddie's been on the right track badgering me," she said. "Things are missing. I guess it's been going on awhile. How would I know when I can't lay my hands on anything?"

He had no idea how to respond, but he couldn't just walk away. So he waited, and when she said no more, he asked, "Want me to look for something?"

"You?" She seemed surprised. Then she shook her head. "No, forget it." She flopped back on the bed.

He waited a moment longer, then slipped out the door. For some reason he found himself running. He couldn't get away from there fast enough.

That night he mentioned at supper that Astrid was upset.

"Upset?" Mom asked him. "What about?"

He shrugged. "Maybe depressed," he amended.

"She's got plenty to be depressed about," Dad remarked.

"She can't find anything anymore," Duncan said.

Mom sighed. "All right. I'll go see what I can do. You guys clean up here."

She came back almost at once.

"Well?" Dad asked.

Mom shook her head. "Astrid's so angry she can't think straight. She told me someone's stealing things."

"Who'd want to take anything from that house?" asked Roz.

Ignoring Roz's jab, Mom said, "She's not making a lot of sense. I think she's just going stir crazy. She's alone too much. And she feels helpless."

Later Duncan heard Mom talking on the phone to Wanda Mattos about getting the neighborhood more involved.

"What neighborhood?" Roz muttered.

Mom heard her as she hung up the receiver. "Wanda said she and Bud will drop in midday tomorrow. Without Mace."

"Do you think Mace still hates her?" asked Duncan.

Roz said, "Doesn't he hate everyone?"

"Roz!" Mom said. "Mace fought for his country. He deserves respect."

Duncan thought about this. Everyone steered clear of Mace because he was unpredictable. Tracy had said it was no picnic around home when he binged, but it wasn't his fault because of the pain he was in and the awful things that had happened to him.

Mom said, "Maybe Doris ought to check in, too. I'll give her a call."

"She'll be there on the weekend," Duncan reminded her.

"I know. But she doesn't usually get there till after she's done the shopping. If she could stop by Friday after work, she might get Astrid involved in planning meals. You know, ask her what she's out of and what she needs. That way she might not feel totally useless."

Duncan saw a chance to free up Friday afternoon. "If Doris goes there tomorrow, she can feed the dog, too," he said.

"Doris won't be there for the dog," Mom said. "Try to be helpful, and don't be grudging."

So much for a break, thought Duncan. He hated coming and going with Astrid there and yet somehow absent. At least Tracy had agreed to help him finish the counting.

On Saturday morning he could hear shouting as he approached the Valentine house. He figured he'd better remind Astrid that he and Tracy would be working in the shed.

"I'm being invaded!" Astrid was yelling at Doris, who was upstairs. "How come everybody thinks they can walk in whenever they want, take whatever they want? What are you doing up there, anyway?"

"I'll be down in a minute," Doris called to her.

"No one's taking anything," Duncan said as he shut the front door behind him. "They're just trying to help."

"What do you know?" Astrid retorted. "You don't know anything."

"Coming," Doris called again as she clumped down the stairs. "Oh, Duncan. I didn't know you were here. I'll see to Mo over the weekend."

"I just stopped to see if it was still all right to have Tracy Mattos help in the shed." He turned from Astrid to Doris. "Mr. Shoop—Eddie—said ..."

"Yes, fine, fine." Astrid waved him out.

Doris followed him to the door. "She's on a tear. I can't tell what's bugging her. She's never acted this ... rude."

"I can hear you!" Astrid bellowed. "Don't think you can all take advantage of me just because of my condition."

"No one's taking advantage," Doris snapped, turning back to the kitchen.

"Then what were you doing upstairs?" Astrid demanded.

"Making up the bed for your nephew. Trying to clean out the spare room."

"Cleaning me out, all right," Astrid muttered.

Duncan shut the door behind him.

Tracy, waiting by the mailbox, said, "What's all the yelling about?"

He shrugged. "She'd better watch out or she'll drive Doris right out of there."

"Maybe she doesn't want me working in the shed," Tracy said.

"I don't know what she wants. Neither does she. Let's just go. We have to keep track of the time. The nephew will pay us when he gets here."

Walking along the overgrown driveway, Tracy said, "My mom

and dad don't think she'll be able to stay all that long, not by herself. It's too bad Doris can't move in with her."

Duncan didn't mention that Astrid had just complained about being invaded.

"There must be a ton of iron out here," Tracy remarked as they passed the rusting stoves.

Duncan glanced at them. It was hard to believe they were worth anything. "Do you remember when the chickens were here?" he asked Tracy.

"Sure. Not exactly. I remember hearing the roosters, and I sort of remember that time she asked for help because something was killing them. Grandpa sent Uncle Mace over with his shotgun. Mom and Dad said that was a mistake, since it was Mace who shot out the salvage sign."

"What happened when he went?" Duncan asked.

"Nothing much. I guess it was okay after all. Mace shot the raccoon or the fox or the coyote, whatever it was. But then it happened again, the killing. By then Dad and Mom had convinced Grandpa that he shouldn't send Uncle Mace. He's sort of a loose cannon, Uncle Mace, even when he isn't mad at someone. Then Mrs. Valentine gave up on the chickens."

As they came to the shed, Duncan glanced over at the sign. Three holes in it, none a bull's-eye.

Tracy stopped beside him. She seemed to guess what he was thinking. "Well, he was probably drunk then, or high. Or both. When he gets like that, he can't even hold a spoon without his hand shaking."

They walked inside and picked up where Duncan had left off. For a while Tracy stuck to the job. But it was too boring not speaking at all.

"If they want to sell this stuff," she said, "they'd better clean it up before anyone comes to look." She blew at the dust that furred the doorknobs in front of her. "See? Customers need to know that what they're looking at is real crystal."

Duncan wasn't sure what she meant by crystal. As far as he could tell, glass was glass. Like the doorknob in his room that he kept forgetting to bring back. While he thought of it, he added another stroke on the lined page to include it in the tally.

Late that afternoon Doris came to the Veericks', her face a storm cloud, her eyes spilling over. "Never," she sobbed. "Never did I think. I've stood by her. Every step of the way. She told Eddie Shoop. First thing after he came in. She told him I'd ... *snitched* things."

Duncan and Roz were drawn to the kitchen, drawn by the spectacle of a grown woman losing it.

Their mother glanced frantically at them, as if they might supply the reassuring words she couldn't summon. But they just stared. And listened.

"She doesn't know what she's saying," Mom finally suggested, but without much conviction. "She'll realize. She'll be sorry. Tomorrow she'll wake up and ... and apologize," she added weakly.

Doris Beasley reached for the paper towels, tore off a section, and blew her nose. She shook her head. "He's been against me all along. He thought I was her cleaning lady. Cleaning lady! I'm her *friend*."

"Of course you are," Mom said soothingly. "Astrid knows that. She's going to feel terrible about this."

"I don't know what to do," Doris whimpered. "I don't know whether to come back or stay away. I mean, how can she get along without me?"

Duncan retreated. After a moment Roz joined him in the living room.

"What's been stolen?" she whispered.

He shrugged. "Nothing I know of. She's always in a snit over losing stuff." He paused, letting his mind run through the most recent grievances. But he couldn't think of anything that would lead to an accusation against Doris. "She counts on Doris to find things," he said. "Maybe she expects too much. She seemed fine last week, but lately she's been acting crazier every day."

As soon as Doris started to leave, Duncan went upstairs. Out of the way, he thought. He dreaded what was bound to follow, Mom sending him over to the Valentine house to be sure everything was all right. He'd lie low, at least until Dad got home. Maybe Dad would have something to talk about that would keep Mom from starting in on Astrid. Anyway, the nephew was there now. Eddie. He'd be taking care of things.

Sunday morning Duncan woke up to the realization that he had to go over to the Valentine house to get paid for the inventory. Or did he? Could Astrid pay him and Tracy later on?

But Astrid hadn't hired him. Eddie Shoop had. And Eddie Shoop was there now.

When Duncan knocked and then let himself in, everything inside the house seemed normal. Mo came charging up to him as though he hadn't seen him in a year, and Astrid ignored him. She was sitting on her bed sorting through a file folder, papers spread all around her.

"Eddie!" She waited a moment and called again. "Eddie, I think I found some of the invoices."

Eddie came in from the living room, brushing past Duncan in

the hall. "Good," he said, "because the other drawer seems to be full of photos and personal stuff."

Duncan moved toward the kitchen, then hesitated. He could see Astrid hold up a piece of paper, and then Eddie was beside her, his back to Duncan. There was nothing to do but wait.

"Oh, well, but this was back in eighty-nine. They might not even be in business anymore. And these prices won't apply now."

"Well," Astrid told him, "it's all I could come up with. Paul wasn't into record keeping."

Eddie shrugged and turned away. "Never mind. I'll wing it." Starting back to the living room, he seemed to notice Duncan for the first time. "Is there a problem?" he asked.

Duncan shook his head. "I finished the inventory. Me and Tracy Mattos."

"Oh, good," said Eddie. "Where'd you leave it?"

Duncan said, "The pad's in the shed. It's all there, everything counted."

"Great," Eddie told him. "That means I can crunch the numbers." He was talking to Astrid now, not Duncan. "I've already had some preliminary bids online. Restoration contractors. You'd be amazed at how the old hardware and trappings are in demand now. It won't take long to clear them out."

He was striding into the living room, leaving Duncan standing in the entrance to the kitchen. "Now that the job's done," Duncan said to Eddie's back, "can you pay us?"

"Oh," said Eddie, turning back to Duncan. "That why you're here?"

Duncan nodded.

"Tell you what," Eddie said. "You bring me the pad with all

the numbers, and I'll see what I can come up with. Unless," he added as if it were an afterthought, "unless you want to wait till the guy comes for the stoves. Then I'll have plenty of cash and I'll probably be feeling a lot more generous."

Duncan was stumped. "You mean, come back later?"

Eddie smiled. "It's a thought. I told Stan Brecher—that's the guy who's picking them up—that Astrid wanted cash, no checks. It's up to you, Duncan," Eddie told him.

"When's he coming?" Duncan asked.

"Around noon," Eddie said.

"Okay. I guess I'll wait," Duncan said, though he wondered why Eddie Shoop couldn't just pay for the work he'd ordered and be done with it.

"Why don't you take the dog out for a walk," Eddie suggested. "Since you're here."

"Oh, pay the boy," Astrid told him. "Pay him."

Eddie shrugged. "I'll have to raid your cash box. You seem to forget what it's costing me each time I fly up here and rent a car, not to mention time off work."

"You don't need to come this often," Astrid retorted. "I can manage the sales. There's plenty of old customers still around. I haven't forgotten how to cut a deal."

Eddie returned to the kitchen, the invoice still in his hand. "I know that, Astrid," he replied. "It's just that you aren't able to make sure that they don't load up stuff they haven't paid for. We'll be done with all this pretty soon. I'll see the stoves on their way, and we might get lucky and find a big-time contractor who'll buy the whole lot. If I can pull that off, it won't matter whether I'm home or here, and you won't have to worry about anyone taking advantage of you while you're laid up."

Astrid nodded. She sighed. "Right. I keep forgetting all you can get done on the Internet. You're doing a terrific job hauling me out of this hole, and I *am* grateful."

"I know. I know you are. And I know it must be hard to be stuck like this when you've always managed. Look at it this way: With the website up and running, we're already getting inquiries. Your sales prospects are real good."

He went back to the living room, leaving Duncan poised midway between the front hall and the kitchen. Had the payment issue been settled? Astrid seemed to think so, since she leaned back and closed her eyes.

Duncan waited a moment. Then he left the house, walking away from his payment, away from Mo, away from Astrid's prospects, whatever they might be.

Duncan crossed the road and walked down to the Mattos house. The Border collie lying on the wraparound porch rose to greet him and then lay back down. Duncan could see Tracy's mother through the open window. He didn't know whether to knock on the door or speak directly to her. He watched her pick up some large bundle, and then she disappeared from view. A moment later the door opened and Mace Mattos stepped out.

"Hello," he said, nodding his nearly bald head. "Waiting for someone?" He sounded perfectly ordinary today.

Duncan, embarrassed, said, "I was just going to knock."

Mace Mattos called inside, "Wanda? It's the Veerick boy." Leaving Duncan standing there, he headed for the barn. The dog got up again and trotted after him.

Wanda Mattos came to the open door. "Oh, Duncan, hi," she said. "Tracy's out back. Want me to give her a shout?"

"Is it all right if I go look for her?" he asked.

"Be my guest. But I hope she's all finished in the Valentine shed."

He nodded. "We're getting paid today." Had he spoken too soon? "I think we are," he added. "After they sell those old stoves."

"Oh, yes?" said Mrs. Mattos with mild surprise. "Doubt they're worth much, except for scrap. They've been out in the weather since long before Paul died."

"The nephew thinks they'll sell well," Duncan said. Was that right? Hadn't Eddie Shoop said as much?

Wanda Mattos shrugged. "And all those doorknobs and hinges and that? From the look of Tracy and her clothes when she came back from there, I'd say they might as well be hauled off to the dump."

"No, no," Duncan protested. "That's what antiques look like before they're cleaned up."

Wanda Mattos shook her head. "Well, it was good of you and Tracy to help out. Astrid could use a hand. We haven't been all that neighborly in recent years like we should've been. Because of an unfortunate incident that happened. I understand you're over there a lot. Being a good neighbor like that, it's beyond the call of duty."

Why was everyone hooked on that duty stuff? And did she mean that he and Tracy shouldn't accept money from Eddie Shoop because they were really helping out Astrid?

Baffled, Duncan said, "I think I'll just get back now."

"Want me to tell Tracy something for you?" asked her mother.

"No, thanks. I'll see her later." He practically ran off the porch. When he got out to the road, he slowed. Then he caught a glimpse of a truck backing into the Valentine driveway. Perfect timing, he thought. Eddie was about to be paid.

Duncan walked up to the front door. By the time he had knocked and let himself in, he found Astrid seated at her desk and talking with a short, wiry man she called Stan. He had straddled the arm of the couch, leaning against its back, and they were laughing together like old friends. Eddie was there, too, but off to one side listening and watching. After a while he inserted himself between them and asked Stan whether he wanted to get the appraisal over with before they loaded up.

"That won't take but a minute," said Stan. "I know the contents of the shed like I know my own warehouse. Let's get the stoves. I brought a ramp and a dolly. I figure it'll take maybe one more trip, but not today. It's almost two hours to home." He rose. "Good to see you up and about, Astrid. I miss the old days, doing business with you and Paul."

Astrid said, "Of course you do, Stan. You always made out like a bandit."

Stan threw back his head and laughed. Then he said, "But you've done all right on your own. I've always said Paul would be proud of you. And now you have your nephew here looking after you big-time."

Duncan started to follow the two men out, but Astrid called him back. "Quick," she said as soon as the men had gone. "I need you to move some things out of here."

Puzzled, he waited for her to go on.

"See those stone sculptures?" She pointed to the walrus figure and the polar bear and the birds and seals.

"What do you want me to do with them?" he asked her.

"Take them away. Out of the house. Put them somewhere safe, out of sight."

Mystified, he crossed the room and picked up the polar bear, which was surprisingly heavy. "Safe how?" he asked. "You want them in the shed?"

"No!" she almost shouted. "No way."

"How about the root cellar?" he asked, thinking of the big bins full of sand.

"Maybe for now," Astrid said. "But as soon as possible, take them away altogether. Do it this coming week. When you're here for Mo."

"Why not Eddie? Won't he help?"

Astrid groaned. "Eddie's in a hurry. Not that I blame him. He's doing his level best to clean out this place and provide for me, which is hard to do long-distance. But these are mine. He doesn't get it. He'll contact people I've never set eyes on, and they'll show up with money I don't need. When I'm ready to part with something I care about, I'll do it my way, with dealers I know."

Duncan carried the stone polar bear through the kitchen and then down the stairs. Mo bounced around him, nearly tripping him up. On his way back for the next stone figure, he shoved Mo out through the dog flap and blocked it. Mo started to bark.

"What's the matter, baby?" Astrid yelled out to the dog.

Duncan explained that Mo was a hazard on the stairs.

Astrid said, "Be careful. Those sculptures, they're irreplaceable, and they're worth a mint."

Back and forth he went until only a few worked stones remained on the shelves in the living room.

"Leave those," Astrid instructed. "I don't want the place stripped bare. That would just call attention to the removal."

Duncan's arms ached. Did she expect him to carry all those heavy stone things back up again to take somewhere else? Where? What did she mean by "safe"? Wouldn't Eddie notice their absence here?

"I think you should go now," she told him. "Before Eddie and Stan Brecher come back in and start asking questions. I can come up with answers of some sort, but it'll be easier if you're not here listening."

Duncan unblocked the dog flap and left through the front door. He was nearly home before it occurred to him that he still hadn't been paid.

Duncan didn't go back to the Valentine house until after supper. He was tempted to ask Tracy to come with him, since she was likely to be more effective with the nephew. But Astrid was too unpredictable these days, and there was no telling how she would react if he brought Tracy along.

Hearing raised voices, he nearly backed off.

"You should tell me things like this," Eddie was shouting.

"I am," Astrid yelled back at him. "That's what I'm doing. But it doesn't have anything to do with you. It's not your problem."

Duncan raised a hand to knock. Tomorrow, maybe? But Eddie would be gone.

"Astrid, listen to me." Eddie's voice dropped, but Duncan could still hear him. "If Stan Brecher asked about mummies, he can't be the only one who's into that sort of stuff. Someone trying to jerk you around could get you in serious trouble."

Now, thought Duncan, while things inside were quieter. He knocked as he opened the door, then stepped into the front hall and stooped down to meet the impact of the hysterical little dog.

Eddie swung around to face him. "I bet even Duncan knows," he said.

Duncan tried to move past him. "I'll feed Mo," he mumbled.

But Eddie forced the issue. "Go ahead, Astrid. Ask him if he knows about them."

Astrid said, "He was a little kid then. He was never around here."

"Try him," Eddie told her.

Astrid said, "Duncan, did you ever hear about us having mummies?"

Duncan didn't have to feign his bewilderment. Had she forgotten about the doll thing? Or was she deliberately steering him away from it? "Mummies?" he repeated, stalling, trying to figure out what she wanted from him.

"That's right. Mummies. We had a slew of them one time. Paul started to sell the lot off, then found out what they were worth, so he held some back to keep them scarce. Did you hear anything about it back then?"

Duncan shook his head.

"See?" Astrid declared, looking back at Eddie. "It's ancient history. So to speak." She beamed at her own cleverness. "We didn't know it was illegal back then. Or else it wasn't. No one worried about it. Anyway, it's all in the past."

"Stan Brecher doesn't seem to think so," Eddie told her. "He says he had a deal going just before Paul died. Then you told him there weren't any left, so he let it go. Now he has a new customer inquiring."

"He's just fishing," Astrid said. "You don't know Stan like I do. He's always angling."

Eddie shook his head and went back to his laptop in the living room.

Duncan looked at Astrid. Now that she had made her point, she had calmed down.

"We'll talk later." She spoke in an undertone. "You'd better feed Mo."

He fed and exercised the dog. By the time he was ready to leave, Eddie had gone upstairs and Astrid was dozing. For the second time that day Duncan went home with empty pockets. He knew Tracy would be annoyed, but he had no idea how to handle the situation.

On Monday morning she fell into step beside him and went straight to the point. "You came over yesterday. What for?"

"I thought we were about to be paid."

"Why didn't you wait for me?"

He shrugged.

"Uncle Mace give you a hard time?"

He shook his head. He said, "I went back to the Valentine house. A guy was there buying stuff. I couldn't … didn't wait."

"Now what?" Tracy asked. "Do we check in on our way home?"

Duncan said, "I don't know if the nephew will still be there. I'm not sure what's going on." He peered down the highway to see if the bus was coming. "I guess I blew it," he told Tracy. "I wasn't there when … when the nephew was free."

"We'll go after school," Tracy said. It wasn't a question or even a suggestion. She intended to make Eddie Shoop or Astrid Valentine settle up.

He turned to face her. Behind him the bus came lumbering along and wheezed to a stop. As usual, they found seats apart.

Looking out the window, he tried to think of an approach that would work. Not bug Astrid, he decided. The trouble was that Tracy didn't care that this was Eddie's deal. Still, her being there might get him off the hook about the stone sculptures, since Astrid wasn't likely to mention them in front of anyone else.

All of this occupied his thoughts through social studies and math. But by third period, which was science, he let it go, his attention focused on the paramecia reproducing in the hay infusion he had started the week before. Duncan counted the magnified creatures, then kept on gazing at them until someone demanded to use the microscope.

At lunchtime kids started talking about spring vacation and ended up griping about summer plans and the lack of available jobs. It wasn't fair that almost anyone in high school, who could work practically anywhere, usually ended up taking the few jobs that were open to kids their age.

"You're all set," Jeb Myers said to Duncan. "You've got an in at the Mattos farm. Your girlfriend will take care of you."

Before Duncan could declare that Tracy wasn't his girlfriend, Neil said, "He's already working at the salvage place."

Jeb asked Duncan what he did and how it paid.

Duncan shot a grateful glance Neil's way and said he helped around the place. Since he was about to get his first pay, he didn't know yet how much it was.

"That should be fixed ahead of time," Jeb told him. "So they can't get out of it."

"They won't," Duncan said with more confidence than he felt. "There's just a lot going on right now. They're selling stuff."

"What, toilet seats?"

Everyone laughed.

"Old stuff," Duncan replied, refusing to rise to the bait. At least the girlfriend talk was over for now.

Getting off the bus behind Tracy, Duncan stepped sideways to avoid looking as though they were together. But of course they were the only kids walking up Garnet Road.

As soon as the bus was on its way, Duncan stopped worrying about appearances. Tracy didn't seem to notice that he'd shunned her. Or maybe she just didn't care. Probably she'd have felt the same way if anyone had suggested he was her boyfriend.

When they came to the farm driveway, he said to Tracy, "If the nephew pays up, I'll stop by with your money."

Tracy shook her head and continued on up the road. Then she stopped. "He's not there," she pointed out. "No car."

Duncan stared at the empty driveway, a riot of fresh green growth except for the muddy ruts left by Stan Brecher's truck. Was Eddie really gone or simply off on an errand? "Sorry," he said. "Astrid may not be able to come up with the money." He felt crummy. Not only had he tried to blow Tracy off, but he'd let her down. "I messed up," he told her.

"No sweat." She grinned. "We'll charge him interest on late payment."

"Well," he said, "I still have to go in there. For the dog," he added.

Tracy nodded, turned, and crossed to the farm side of the road.

The inside of the Valentine house looked trashed. It was far worse than the last time the nephew had left it. Cartons, file folders, and drawers with overflowing contents occupied all the available floor space as well as other surfaces.

Mo, at the far end of the living room, came skidding over papers that fanned out from fallen stacks that might have hinted at some previous attempt at order.

"Oh, good," said Astrid, looking up from her desk, which was piled high with boxes and baskets, themselves full of smaller objects. "Take Mo outside before he wrecks my organization."

Duncan's gaze swept the room. One small dog couldn't have created all this chaos. He glanced at Astrid, who scowled as she turned over pages in a scruffy notebook. Then he led Mo into the kitchen and over to the dog door. As soon as Mo was shoved out, he popped right back through.

"Later," Duncan said. "I'll come later." This time Mo resisted, but Duncan was quick to block the flap, leaving the dog whining pitifully on the back porch.

From the front hall he surveyed the living room again. Who was going to clean up this mess? "Is Eddie gone?" he asked Astrid.

"For the moment," she replied. Then she shifted awkwardly, unable to turn enough to face him directly. Still, she commanded his full attention. "That's why you have to finish removing those sculptures. Right away, Duncan. Out of the cellar, away from here."

"Why?" he asked.

"Because Eddie's in a swivet over the really valuable objects, especially if they might've been imported illegally. He's convinced Paul was trafficking in protected goods, like carved ivory, that kind of thing. He still plans to cash in on the Eskimo stuff, but he can't until he's sure the record is clean. Right now he's trying to track down where everything came from. He says I mustn't sell any of it yet. He doesn't hear me when I tell him it's not for sale."

Duncan said, "Isn't he mostly afraid someone might walk off with things?"

"That too," Astrid said. "Especially now that he's advertising on the Internet. Of course strangers could swipe outside artifacts the way Doris helped herself to inside treasures. But Eddie's also afraid that someone like Stan Brecher, who knows the ropes, could force us to sell cheap. You know, threaten to report us. Now, I don't go along with him on that. Paul and I dealt with Stan and the others for years. If it was illegal for one of us, it was illegal for the rest. Paul never set out to break the law. He just took care of business. But Eddie's new at all this. He doesn't know the dealers like I do. And he's Mr. Clean when it comes to rules and regulations. He'd flip his lid if he knew about the leftover mummy."

So Astrid still hadn't told her nephew. How did she expect to keep it from him?

Astrid straightened, resting her hands on her knees. "In a way," she said, "I wish Eddie had never come to help. Oh, he's been wonderful, but he's too much of a worrier. He claims the new insurance will pay for itself, but I can't see how. And look at this house. It's been turned inside out."

"You need Doris," Duncan told her.

"Huh!" Astrid grunted. "You don't know what she's been up to."

Duncan said, "She's really upset. She says she never took anything from you."

"You'd know the truth if you'd heard what she said when I asked her about the old bones. Sure, she pretended to look for them. But she acted like she didn't know they were special. Now there's only a few of them left. The rest are nowhere to be found."

"Bones?" Puzzled, Duncan was almost afraid to ask what Astrid meant. A mummy was one thing. But if there was a skeleton, too, what was she doing with it here?

Astrid nodded. "Very rare. Very old. One of our buyers was crazy for them. He had a client that was a big collector. I think he had a museum connection." She sighed. "And now, who knows where they are."

Wait a minute—bones. There had been bones behind the sofa. Between the sofa and the bookcase. "I saw them," Duncan said. "I didn't know what they were. I mean, I figured you didn't want Mo chewing on them."

"Where?" Astrid tried to push herself up and out of the chair. She reached for her walker. "When did you see them?"

Duncan wasn't sure when. Before Astrid came home from the rehab center, anyway.

On her feet at last, Astrid shuffled through the clutter and then turned to survey the living room. "Mo was chewing on them? How did he get them?"

Duncan said, "I don't know. Some were on the floor and some on the bottom shelf of the bookcase." He pointed to the far wall. "Where the couch used to be."

As he spoke, the scene returned to him, the bone figure slimy from Mo's mouth, the other ones so strangely shaped and so pitted. Weird! he'd thought. Then he'd gathered them up and ... and stuck them higher, behind a stack of books.

"There!" he told her, beginning to shove aside boxes and stepping over piles of folders to reach the shelf with the books lying on their sides. "There," he repeated, pulling some books and reaching behind others. He brought out the carved bones, one after another. Two were already badly chewed. "Now you can tell Doris," he said.

"Tell her what?" Astrid snapped.

"That you're sorry you accused her. Maybe she'll come back next weekend and clean all this up for you."

"I'm not sorry. There's more missing than those. Of course I'm glad you found them. It's a big relief, though they'll have to be hidden, too. You'd better get going with the stone sculptures. I'm thinking you could dig a hole somewhere safe for now. Not the bones; they'd be eaten. Still, you need to get them off this property before Eddie decides to put them up for sale, too. Somewhere dry. Duncan, did you hear me? Then we deal with the mummy."

Duncan shook his head. He'd stopped by to take care of the dog and pick up the money he and Tracy had earned. Now Astrid was ordering him to work some more, this time for her, and she'd barely thanked him for rescuing those bone things, let alone acknowledged that she had mistakenly accused Doris of stealing them.

"First we need to call Doris," he said.

"Doris is at work," Astrid retorted. "And what I need to do and what you need to do are entirely separate things."

What had become of their level meeting ground? Was this her true self, fully recovered? If it was, Duncan would quit. The invalid Astrid, even when difficult, had been bearable. This tyrant was not.

Yet he couldn't just walk away. Glumly he went down to the

cellar to start lugging the stone sculptures back upstairs and out to the porch until he could figure out where to bury them.

Mo, released from banishment, cavorted around his feet, ecstatic in his company and oblivious of the stone figures that collected outside his door flap.

Duncan carried a few of the stone figures to the fence and dropped them over. When one of them struck another, he stopped. Astrid would have a fit if any got chipped or even scratched.

He vaulted the gate, passed the door to the shed, and crossed the driveway, which looked spacious now with most of the stoves gone. Two remained, though. Could he hide the sculptures in them? No one would look inside those rusting hulks. But what if Stan Brecher came back and took the stoves away in his truck?

Duncan waded through last year's brambles and fresh green nettles that overspread the entrance to the chicken house. The door, though no longer hooked, refused to yield to him. Who in their right mind would come here and brave the sagging chicken wire festooned with creeping vines? It was a perfect hiding place for now. Maybe later on he could dig a hole for the sculptures in what used to be the coop.

He climbed through a broken window and struggled again with the door, which he couldn't budge. Not that it mattered much. Astrid's precious stuff would be safe here. He scanned the inside through crisscrossed splinters of light from countless cracks in the flimsy walls. Dried droppings covered everything, so that when he walked, the floor crunched beneath his feet. Ducking spiderwebs and dusty roosts, he eyed the nesting boxes and imagined a walrus in one, a polar bear or a hunter in another. What could be neater? Even the bone things could be stashed here, couldn't they?

Back and forth he went, his arms too burdened with the stone sculptures to fend off the prickly tangle of last year's blackberry canes amid the supple new red creepers and the stinging nettles. With every return trip for more stones, he whacked and trampled his way out. By the time he had finished bringing all the figures to the chicken house and had stuffed them into nesting boxes, he was fed up with this whole stupid project. The sour reek of chicken manure was in his nostrils and probably on his clothes. He would feed the dog and go home.

Astrid was on her bed when he came inside with Mo. "You took your time," she remarked. "You've got to clear out the bones before we can deal with the mummy."

"No," he said, setting down the dog food and then filling the water bowl. "No, I have to go. I've got homework."

"You can't just walk away!" Astrid exclaimed. "You'll leave those things exposed."

"Maybe tomorrow," he said without much conviction. If it weren't for the dog, he'd never come back.

"Duncan," she said. "Please. I'd do it myself if I could."

Now he was supposed to pity her because she couldn't get around the way she used to. He stood his ground, though, barely nodding in response.

"I didn't tell you this before," she continued. "I'm afraid some- thing's going on. Might be going on. It's not just Eddie being wor- ried about those people he's already contacted over the Internet. He had to tell them our location because they want to come and look things over. That's supposed to be by appointment, but he let slip that he's not available most weekdays. You see?"

Duncan nodded again. He felt like asking her why Eddie hadn't put away the most valuable items himself. He knew the stone figures existed. They'd been all over the living room. Probably he'd already listed some of them on his website.

"Listen, Duncan," she said, her tone almost pleading. "Take the bones home with you. They'll be safe at your house. Besides, I'd like you to keep one. They're rare, those worked bones. You deserve something special after all you've done for me. Go ahead and pick one and then put the rest away until I'm on my feet again. Please, Duncan."

He relented. Not because she wanted to give him one of them. He'd have preferred a stone sculpture, but he didn't think he could say so. Instead he told her that she didn't have to give him anything, which only made her insistent.

"Bring those over here," she ordered as he began to stuff them into a grocery bag. "Come on, Duncan. This won't take long."

After he dumped the carved bones beside her, she spread them out and asked him which he liked best. When he shrugged, she held up a vertebra shaped into an owl with outstretched wings. "How about this?" she asked. She darted a look at him. "I can see it doesn't thrill you. Maybe you'll change your mind about it later on. If you don't, well, you can always sell it. I suspect it'll bring a pretty penny."

He thanked her and finished packing up the bone figures in a couple of grocery bags. After all, it was no big deal to ease her mind this way. He'd carry them up the road to his house and stash them in the downstairs closet for now.

He was on his way out when Astrid spoke up again. "You'll come tomorrow?" She sounded anxious, almost frightened. "You'll come and get the mummy out of here?"

He wanted to shout *No!* He wanted to tell her enough was enough. But he found himself trying to explain that he couldn't deal with the mummy by himself. "If I can ask Tracy Mattos to help," he said. "She's strong. She might even find some place for it in the barn."

"Will she talk about it?" Astrid demanded.

"Of course not," Duncan retorted. How should he know? Well, actually he supposed she might. But how did Astrid know *he* wouldn't talk?

"All right, then," Astrid said with a sigh. She sounded as though he had driven a hard bargain and she had caved in out of desperation. "Don't be late, though," she added as he deposited the bags of bones outside the door and shut it behind him.

He hoisted his backpack and picked up the bags. One more day, he promised himself, and then he would be finished with Astrid. Done.

Once he was home and changed into clothes that didn't reek of the chicken house, he realized that quitting Astrid Valentine wasn't as simple as his resolve. He needed to convince his parents.

As soon as he heard their car drive up to the house, he went downstairs, poised to say whatever it took to bring them around. He could hear them arguing about the upcoming town meeting as they came inside.

"I can't do Astrid Valentine anymore," Duncan blurted. "She's crazy. She acts like I'm her slave."

His parents broke off their argument. Then his father said, "Duncan, can't this wait?"

"It's important!" Duncan retorted.

"No need to shout," said his mother.

"It's important," he repeated, lowering his voice. "She gets worse and worse. Doris Beasley knows. Ask her."

His father said, "I'm sure it's tough on you. And you've been a terrific help. Why don't we try to work out some other system for Astrid. We'll talk to the nephew—"

"He's gone away again," Duncan said.

"All right. We'll talk to him when he comes back."

"You mean I'm done there?" Duncan asked.

"I just said," his father replied. "We'll talk to the nephew and explain that you have to pull back. We know there's a lot of extra activities in school this time of year, plus graduation. But right now we can't leave Astrid in the lurch, especially after the rift with Doris. It's only a few more days, Duncan. Then you'll be out of there."

"There's a mummy," Duncan said.

"Let's talk about all of this after supper," his mother told him. "Okay? Your dad and I are in the middle of something."

Duncan went back up to his room. He guessed he'd made some headway. Well, he'd have to show up at Astrid's for the next few days. But tomorrow he'd have Tracy along. Astrid had agreed to that. Would Tracy come? The Valentine house fascinated her. Besides, the mummy ought to be a lure. If it was a mummy. He still hadn't inspected it, but Astrid seemed convinced that it was.

He was tempted to call Tracy, to make sure he could count on her. But he could hear himself explaining and Tracy yelping, "Mummy? Did you say mummy?" Anyone in her house would hear her, and that would be the end of Astrid's secret.

In spite of everything, it still was a secret, because even though he'd announced the mummy's existence, his parents hadn't seemed to hear him, or else they'd misunderstood. Later on, when they got around to discussing Astrid, he'd just tell them about the mess in her house and her fear of being ripped off.

But there wasn't any discussion, because Roz came home in tears, on the verge of breaking up with Denny. Despite her insistence that she didn't want to talk about it, she kept storming up to her room and then coming back down to call a friend. The household was charged with tension, the rest of the family intent on keeping out of her way.

Eventually Duncan settled down to his homework.

At the bus stop Tuesday morning Duncan asked Tracy if she could help him after school.

"At Valentines'?" she asked.

He nodded. He didn't want to get into it yet.

"Something else we're supposed to be paid for?"

"Don't worry," he said. "We'll be paid. The nephew's got a lot on his mind. He's trying to wrap things up so he doesn't have to keep coming all the time."

"If it's in that shed—" she began to protest.

"No," he quickly assured her. "In the house. Something important." As Roz approached, walking briskly but refusing to run, Duncan said, "No one else knows about it."

"Tell me," Tracy said to him.

"I will," he said. "Later," he added, dropping his voice.

After school when, finally, they were on the road home with no Roz, he told Tracy what he knew about the mummy.

"Wait a minute," Tracy said. "You mean you're not exactly sure it's a mummy?"

"Well, I'm sort of sure. I mean, Astrid is. It's dug in pretty deep. Anyhow, if that's what it is, it'll be worth a whole lot more than all that stuff we counted that the nephew's already getting bids on. Astrid wants it stowed away somewhere off her property."

At the front door Tracy hung back until Duncan announced

their arrival and quieted the yapping dog. Then she followed him into the kitchen, where Astrid reclined on her hospital bed surrounded by folders and envelopes with papers spilling out of them.

"Better get right to it," Astrid ordered.

"Hello, Mrs. Valentine," Tracy said.

Astrid nodded and mumbled something.

Duncan pushed Mo out the dog flap and blocked it. Then he started for the cellar door. But Tracy stayed put.

"You going with him?" Astrid demanded.

"Maybe," Tracy answered. "First I want to know when we get paid."

"Tracy!" Duncan exclaimed. "I told you—"

"Paid for what?" Astrid demanded.

"For all the counting we did out in the shed. Duncan's done much more than me," Tracy added.

Duncan froze. All he needed now was for Astrid to kick Tracy out and leave him on his own here.

"You got paid. Didn't you? Oh, no. Eddie told me to." She glanced over at Duncan, who had turned back from the cellar door. She looked at Tracy standing in the hall at the entrance to the kitchen. "Did I forget?" All the starch had drained from her voice. "Duncan?"

He stepped toward the bed. He shook his head.

"Oh, hell. I guess I was supposed to. I thought it was done." Some of the bluster was returning, though it sounded forced. She leaned over, propping her head with the fingers of her left hand. "Eddie left money," she muttered. "I just have to think where."

Feeling her discomfiture, Duncan tried to shrug off any urgency about it.

But Tracy wasn't about to let this go. "Want me to look for you?" she asked.

Astrid raised her head and nodded. "Try the living room. He had his laptop there. His computer. He was getting bids on all the hardware, just from estimates he made while he was still in New Jersey. He set a ridiculous starting price, way high. He'd already printed out some early bids. You find those and you're bound to find money."

Striding into the living room, Tracy began to wade through the clutter.

Astrid whispered to Duncan, "In here. The fridge. Lower drawer."

What did she want now? he wondered.

"Get on with it," she told him. "It's Eddie's home bank."

Duncan opened the refrigerator door and pulled out the vegetable drawer. "Carrots," he said. "Lettuce and tomatoes. The tomatoes are moldy."

"Underneath," she directed. "Hurry! It's where Eddie hid cash for me."

Rummaging beneath the limp lettuce, he felt something flat and hard. He drew it out, a packet wrapped in plastic, and took it to her.

She fumbled with it, then told him to open it. "How much?" she asked after he handed it back. She pulled one bill after another from the packet. "Eddie told me, but I forget. This keeps happening. I think I've taken care of something, and then it's gone from my mind."

"Wow!" declared Tracy from the living room. "Is this for real? You won't believe the prices on that crap we counted."

"Does thirty each sound right?" asked Astrid. "Or were you supposed to get extra?"

Duncan said, "That's fine."

Astrid was counting out money when Tracy declared that there was no sign of actual cash. She started to ease her way out of the living room mess.

Clasping the bills in her fist, Astrid pressed the packet back into Duncan's hand. "Put it away," she ordered. Then, raising her voice, she called to Tracy, "Never mind. It was here all along. I've got it."

Tracy walked over to the bed and took what Astrid proffered.

"You, too, Duncan," Astrid told him. "Here's yours. Funny, I really did think I'd taken care of it. Then I couldn't even remember where Eddie left it."

Duncan said, "I know" and "Thanks" and "It's okay" in rapid succession. All he wanted was to get away from Astrid's lies, even if it meant dealing with the mummy in the root cellar.

"Wait," said Tracy at the bottom of the cellar stairs. "I want to see what she gave me." Under a dangling light-bulb, she counted out a ten and a twenty. "I guess that's okay so far. What about you?"

Grasping the flashlight in one hand, Duncan stuffed the bills into his pocket. "The same, I think," he said. "Let's get done here." He led the way to the root cellar.

"Still," Tracy told him, "if the nephew's anywhere near right about what he thinks he can sell all that stuff for, he ought to double our wages."

Duncan felt like telling her to knock it off. He had to be careful. Even now she could just walk away from the job ahead.

The cavelike atmosphere hit them as they entered. If absolute darkness possessed an odor, this was what it would be like.

Tracy said, "This place is creepy. Isn't there a light?"

Duncan played the flashlight beam above them, located the string, and yanked it.

"Better," Tracy said, "but I still don't like it."

He led the way past the big containers to the one near the end. The light from the single bulb barely reached here. Still, the flash-light revealed the top of the head he had left exposed.

Tracy sucked in her breath. "It's real," she whispered. Then: "Are you sure it's real?"

He shoved the flashlight at her and began to scoop sand away from the figure. "I thought it was some kind of giant doll," he admitted. "I didn't know about any mummies then."

He had to step onto the pallet to hike himself up and partway over the edge of the crate. Now he used both hands as spades. But the sand was so dry it kept filling the hollows he made. "More light," he said, grunting as the top edge of the crate bit into his stomach.

"God!" Tracy exclaimed. "It's got teeth! Look at the teeth!"

"Help," said Duncan, shifting back for a rest. "Maybe we need a shovel."

"Let me try," Tracy said, handing him the flashlight. It wasn't as easy for her to push herself up, but once she was suspended over the crate, she tore away at the sand as if her life depended on it. "You too," she said. "We each take a side. Then we pull."

As they scooped away sand, the flashlight kept rolling, leaving them in darkness. Each time Duncan's arm brushed up against the mummy, he started to recoil and had to force himself to scrape and pile the sand.

Then Tracy said that they needed to hoist the mummy up. Duncan didn't protest. Somehow Tracy was in charge now, and that was a relief.

"Fireman's carry," she said.

Duncan tunneled down until he could feel something on the backs of his hands. He shoved his hands through, and after a moment found one of Tracy's.

But leaning over as they were, they couldn't raise the mummy from the sand.

"We've got to stand inside," he said.

"No," she objected. "We'll just move the sand back."

They argued, then compromised. Duncan, the lighter and shorter of them, clambered over the edge of the crate. Stooping low, he found the channels he'd made beneath the mummy. But they were closing in, and it took some effort to meet Tracy's hands across from his.

Raising the mummy out of its bed of sand took all his strength. He could hear Tracy gasp, but neither of them wasted breath on speech. As the sand loosened, he felt the mummy begin to shift. All at once it came free, surprising Duncan with its weight. By himself he could never have lifted it over the edge of the crate, let alone carried it across the cellar and up the stairs.

Tracy said, "Aah," and fell backward. It didn't matter that their hands had parted. Their quarry was perched on top of the sand.

Duncan groped for the flashlight. Finally he was able to play the beam over and around the mummy. He saw long, coarse black hair. Some of it was braided. He saw eye sockets. Were the eyes still there? He saw knees almost jutting through red-brown wrappings and wizened hands and one exposed foot, the toenails all in a row like kernels of dried corn.

"It really is a human being," Tracy whispered with awe. "Shouldn't it be buried?"

He knew what she meant, but he couldn't help saying, "It was. Till we dug it out." Then he began to laugh. She laughed, too, both of them close to hysteria.

When they were able to stop, they set about hoisting the mummy over and down from the raised crate. They seemed to agree that this long-dead human being was somehow fragile and must be dealt with gently.

The way you would treat someone you knew, thought Duncan.

Sweat and sand stuck to him as he kept the mummy from dropping heavily while Tracy on the outside eased it down. When he finally climbed out, drenched and chilled, he couldn't bear to touch it again. Not yet.

"Upstairs?" Tracy exclaimed. "You're kidding!"

Duncan nodded. Why did she think they had gone to all this trouble to dig it out of the sand? "Not just upstairs, but away from the house. Somewhere out of sight."

Tracy groaned. "It *was* out of sight. No one knew it was there."

"Look," Duncan told her, "Astrid's got her reasons. She wants it off the premises before …" He broke off. If only he could tell Tracy everything. But what if she told her mother and father? It was safer if she didn't know that selling it might be illegal.

"Before what?" Tracy demanded. "Come on, Duncan. If you don't level with me, I'm quitting." She looked down at the huddled figure bound in its woven wraps. "I don't need this. Not even for more money. Normal people don't do this sort of thing. It'll probably give me nightmares."

"I know," Duncan said, averting his eyes from the mummy. "I don't even like touching it. And I know it's not normal, but it's here. Astrid's afraid that if … if the wrong person … people find out about it, she'll be in trouble. It's worth a lot if she can sell it, and she thinks there are people she can contact who know other people who will pay a lot for it. But if the wrong people …" He was floundering now that he had started to spill the beans.

"You mean she thinks someone might steal it?" Tracy asked.

That too, Duncan thought. He nodded. "She needs it out of here, and I can't move it by myself."

"Why didn't she think of this before the nephew left?"

"He's part of the problem," Duncan told her. He wanted to level with her, but all he said was, "It's complicated. It has to do with … with the law."

"What law?" Tracy demanded.

"I don't know!" he almost shouted. "How should I know? Can't we just get the job done and let her worry about all that?"

"What's taking so long?" Astrid bellowed from the kitchen. "What are you kids doing down there?"

They exchanged guilty glances.

"Answer her," Tracy prompted.

"We're trying to figure out how to get it upstairs," Duncan called back to Astrid.

Tracy said, "Let's put it in something. Then we won't have to touch it."

That was fine with Duncan if they could find such a something. They looked over the cellar. The cleaned section offered nothing. But when Tracy kicked around in the messy part, she came up with an old plywood gate that must have been part of a pen. Together they managed to raise and then slide the mummy onto the gate. Now at least they could get a firm grip on the edges of the plywood. They shuffled toward the stairway.

"I'll go backward," Duncan offered. He swiveled and lowered the hinged corner of the gate onto the first step. After clambering around and up to the next step, he stooped and raised it, but too suddenly. Tracy, still maneuvering her end, lost her grip on it. The mummy slid down.

"No!" she cried. "Get it off me!" In a panic, she dropped to her knees and thrust the mummy upward. With one hand clinging to his end, Duncan reached and grabbed the mummy. As the balance shifted back, Tracy seized the lower end of the gate and pushed hard. At the same time she scrambled clumsily to her feet.

With the mummy more or less righted, they moved their burden cautiously, a step at a time. Duncan had to feel his way, one foot stabbing backward at each stair riser to locate the next tread. Then all at once there wasn't any. He realized he had reached the landing. Glancing over his shoulder, he saw the open door.

"Okay?" he asked Tracy. Neither had spoken since the near disaster at the bottom of the stairs.

She grunted something, then said clearly, "Hold on!"

"I am," he told her, backing slowly past the washing machine and then turning in to the kitchen.

Together they set the gate with its burden down on the floor.

"Gross!" Tracy exclaimed. "I never want to see that thing again."

From her bed Astrid said, "Gross? Try treasure. I believe the last one brought twenty-five thousand."

Tracy moved away from the mummy before she replied. "Dollars?"

"Dollars. Cash."

"Is that what you'll get for this?" Tracy asked her.

"Don't know. If it isn't hidden somewhere safe, I won't get anything."

"Why would anyone want to own it?" Tracy asked.

"Old things," Astrid replied. "Some people make a career out of old things. All kinds of people. One customer was into ancient Inca textiles. Another collected skulls. If you've got something rare, you've got a sale. Like I said, Eddie, my nephew, already has unbelievable opening bids on our fixtures. They're small potatoes compared with this."

"Well," Tracy declared, brushing off her hands, "I'm finished. I'm out of here."

"That's fine," Astrid replied, "so long as you take it with you."

Tracy started to laugh. She said, "I'm too big to play with dolls."

"Off the premises," Astrid continued, unfazed. She glanced out the window. "Though maybe you should leave it here till it gets dark. Meanwhile you can scope out your barn or one of the sheds. Plan ahead."

Shaking her head, Tracy started for the door.

"Well, don't leave it there!" Astrid told her. "It's in my way to the bathroom."

Without another word,Tracy returned and helped Duncan slide the gate toward the front hall. They had to stop to shove the hospital bed out of the way.

"Unlock the wheels," Astrid instructed. "Don't you kids think before you act?"

"If I'd thought ahead," Tracy replied, "I wouldn't be here."

"Well, now you are, and you've done a helpless old woman a big favor. So don't be rude about it. And come back later to finish the job," Astrid called after the departing girl.

Duncan replaced the bed and locked the wheels. Then he dashed to the front door, hoping to catch Tracy before she escaped.

Already across the road, Tracy paused to wave before hurrying down the hill to her driveway. He had a feeling she had no intention of checking out the barn.

Duncan didn't go after Tracy. He wanted to get home, find something to eat, decompress.

The telephone was ringing as he walked into his house. The moment he heard Astrid's voice he regretted answering it. She berated him for leaving Mo outside and supperless. She complained about Wanda's rudeness, which baffled him. It couldn't be more than five minutes since he'd left Astrid's. What had Tracy's mother been up to?

"Duncan? Are you there?"

He nodded, then said, "I just got in. I didn't forget about Mo." Accustomed to being truthful, he was surprised at how easily the lie came to him. "I had to do something here. We spent a long time moving that mummy. I'll be back soon." Astrid was still talking as he put down the phone.

He poured his dad's junk cereal into a large bowl, added milk, and began to shovel it into his mouth. Where had such hunger come from? Did the mummy business bother him more than he'd thought? Or was he simply worn out from all the heaving and lugging?

He was more doubtful than ever that there was any point to this huge effort. Why not just level with Eddie and get his help? Even if he was the straight-arrow guy Astrid said he was, he'd still want to protect her and her treasure. If she hadn't done anything wrong, why not just clear out the stuff that could embarrass her or get her in trouble?

Duncan reached for the cereal box, then stopped. He wasn't really hungry anymore. He just wanted to put off returning to the Valentine house and the mummy.

He went up to his room, opened his backpack, and dumped its contents onto his bed. Homework later, he thought. He still had some trumpet time left. Wondering vaguely why Roz wasn't home yet, he picked up the instrument and fluttered his lips the way Mr. Simon had taught him to do before playing.

The last time Mr. Simon had caught up with him at school he had sounded more impatient than puzzled by Duncan's continued absence from band practice. Duncan, who had already explained his situation, assured Mr. Simon that he was about to be freed up. These last few months had been a drag, he said, and he couldn't wait for the whole deal to end.

Mr. Simon hadn't exactly promised to resume lessons, but he'd said he looked forward to getting Duncan back on track.

Duncan blew a few notes, played some scales that squealed in the upper register, and set the trumpet down on top of his homework. Who was he kidding? Even if he played catchup now that he was going to have time for lessons, the most he could hope for was to get back into rehearsals and perform at the end of the year. Well, yes, he might still make it into the band next year at Woodford Valley Regional. But what did that amount to compared with the music he'd heard on Astrid's scratchy tapes? How that trumpet playing astounded him. He might as well go back to buzzing paper on a comb. Blue jay squawks. That was his speed.

He decided to get Astrid and Mo over with now. Then he could concentrate on homework after supper, which would be early tonight since his parents were going to town meeting.

Outside again, he saw that the day had gone gray. Tree frogs shrilled from the lowland woods, a sure sign of rain. That might change Astrid's plans for moving the mummy. He hurried on. He heard Mo yapping in the back yard. Poor idiot dog. Couldn't Astrid bestir herself and reach the door flap? He supposed he'd blocked it too effectively. Even leaning down from her walker, Astrid might not be able to shove the boot box aside.

He began to run. If that yapping was grating to him up here on the road, it must be driving Astrid crazy. Well, crazier than she already was.

He pounded up to her front door. Thrusting it wide, he came face to face with the draped figure huddled in the front hall. It stopped him cold. He didn't think that a mere skeleton would have such an impact. But this dead human was so nearly fleshed that it drew him into its presence as if demanding something or beseeching him.

He reached toward it, ready now to feel the bony foot that had repelled him when he had first set eyes on it. The skin he touched felt like dried bark. He pulled back and stared, first at the eye sockets, which weren't entirely empty, and then at the gaping mouth. The teeth seemed grotesquely prominent. With so many intact, he supposed that this person must have been young. He had no idea whether the long hair with the braids signified female. Whatever this mummy had been was a mystery. It wasn't his business.

Then what was important about it? Not where it ended up, he supposed. What mattered was that it had lived, had been someone. After it died, it had been positioned and wrapped for burial. Only that wasn't the end of it, because it had been taken from its grave and its homeland. So why did that matter—because it was against some law, or because a person had become an object with a price on it?

He and Roz had watched a few horror movies with mummies rising from their tombs. Movie mummies were too out there to be scary. This real one had already lost its creepy aura. Maybe that was because of the way it clutched itself in death.

"Well?" Astrid called to him, her voice querulous, aggrieved.

Duncan roused himself from his scrutiny of the mummy and went into the kitchen, where Astrid, seated on the edge of the bed, leaned forward precariously to take hold of the walker. Duncan stepped close to brace the frame as she slid heavily down to it. She gasped, then straightened. Aware of the effort it took for her to shift from bed to walker, he assumed that she was heading for the bathroom, and he backed toward the hall.

She shook her head, saying, "I want a look at my treasure before you take it away."

He started to tell her that he didn't know where to take it and that anyway he couldn't move it alone. Instead he just went to unblock the dog flap and let Mo in.

Even after he was fed, the little dog kept leaping and twirling, beside himself with joy at being rescued. Finally he scampered through the kitchen to look for Astrid, skidded into the hall, and began to bark furiously.

"No, no!" Astrid commanded, laughing. Then, louder, "*No!* Duncan, help!"

By the time Duncan got to the hall, Mo already had a fold of ancient Peruvian weaving between his teeth. Duncan pried open Mo's jaws to extract the precious textile. This merely freed the dog for a fresh assault on Astrid's treasure. Duncan caught him up and carried him into the kitchen, where he was stuck with the squirming little beast in his arms while he waited for Astrid to take charge.

She finally shuffled back to him. "Did Wanda find a place for it?" she demanded.

Wanda again. So she must mean Tracy. Not bothering to correct her, he said he didn't know. He asked, "What do you want me to do with Mo?"

Astrid shrugged. "Put him out in the yard, I guess."

"But he's just come in. He was barking."

"Then get the mummy out of here." She glanced through the window. "It's getting dark enough now. And no one's around to see."

"It's about to rain," he told her. "Isn't that bad for the mummy?"

She nodded. "Of course it is. They need to be dry. They've lasted for hundreds of years because they've been dry."

"Well, it'll get wet now," he said.

"You're stalling," she replied.

They stood facing one another, at odds. He could feel the dog beginning to relax in his grip, to surrender.

"Just get it out," Astrid told him. "Before the dog eats it or the rain turns it to rot."

Once again Duncan saw that he was trapped, overwhelmed by her helplessness, her craziness, her absolute command of a world only she defined and inhabited.

He waited until Astrid had regained the bed. Then he handed Mo to her. "Keep hold of his collar," Duncan told her.

"I know what to do," she retorted.

He went into the hall to deal with the mummy. He figured if he could just get it outside, then he could go after Tracy. If he swiveled the gate lengthwise, it would fit through the doorway, but there wasn't room for it and him at the same time. First he opened the door as wide as it allowed. The gate turned easily because of the small rug beneath it. He could use another like it, maybe two.

In the living room he shoved aside cartons to free up the rug in front of the couch. Then he surveyed the surrounding clutter and decided one small rug would have to do. Back in the hall, he spread it in front of the threshold and dragged the gate up to it. Then he tried raising the gate with its burden. It was too heavy. He stared at it. If only Tracy were here. He thought some more. Then he shoved the mummy as far back as he could. This time when he struggled to lift the front edge, the gate actually budged.

He was so pleased with this result that he almost forgot to reposition the mummy in the center of the gate. He told himself to take it slowly now. He mustn't tip the gate back too far or lower the front of it too steeply. Either extreme and the mummy would be dumped off.

He glanced over his shoulder hoping to catch sight of Tracy returning. But the road was empty. He tugged the gate until it crossed the threshold. After that it slid more freely, and he found himself holding it back while using all his strength to keep it nearly level until, finally, it was resting outside on the broad granite step.

When he let go, his trembling arms refused to unbend. He had to shake them out. He began to feel the strain in his shoulders now, then in his neck. He sat down beside the mummy. Once again he stared at the road. He didn't care who came along now, his parents or anyone else. He didn't care who helped with this impossible errand. He just wanted it finished.

He was still sitting there when Mo came hurtling out to him. Almost at once Astrid began to call, and he was reminded of that day months ago when he'd found her chasing hopelessly after the dog. He supposed that if he had to do it all over again, he would have to come to her aid. But how different things would be now if he hadn't been on his way home just then. And how clueless he'd been when she and this dog had snared him.

He walked back inside with the dog dancing around his feet. Before closing the door, he said to Astrid, "I'm going to look for Tracy to help with the mummy."

"No. Wait," Astrid called back to him. "I don't want anyone else to know."

"She already does know," he told her. "She helped me get it upstairs. You asked her to find a safe place to hide it."

"Who?" Astrid asked. "Oh, that's right, yes. I hardly know what I've said. I guess I'm just too anxious."

"It's okay," he responded as he closed the door behind him. All in all, he preferred Astrid the tyrant to this pitiable model.

Marveling at the way she could shift from victim to bully and back again, the view of her as witch, with Mo her familiar, slid into focus. Even if she wasn't quite as skillful at it these days, the power she summoned to bring off these transformations seemed like second nature to her.

He ran to the Mattos farm. Tracy came to the door and told him they were having an early supper, because her parents were going to the special town meeting.

"We've got to move the mummy," he whispered. "Did you find a place?"

Tracy shook her head. "Not going to," she told him. "I'm not going near it again."

"It's outside," he told her. "It'll be rained on. I don't know what to do."

"Nothing," she advised. "Try nothing. Stop being the Chicken Lady's slave."

Knowing that Tracy was right did no good. "I just need to get it under cover," he pleaded. How could he explain what he only dimly understood? "It's like a promise," he said. "I have to finish."

"I'm going to show Duncan something," Tracy called to her family. "I'll be right back." She led him behind the milk room to the machine shed. "I'd offer you the four-wheeler," she told him, "but I'd catch hell from Uncle Mace. Try the stone boat," she said, going to the side wall to pull down a sort of low-lying trailer with two small wheels at one end. She dragged it outside. "No one uses it much," she said, "but bring it back sometime."

He must have looked bewildered as well as bleak, because she stayed another minute to demonstrate its use. First she heaved a log onto the stone boat and rolled it back to the rear riser.

"Counterweight," she said. Grasping the hitch, she lifted the front of the stone boat with apparent ease. When she pulled it, the two small wheels at the rear squealed as they turned, but turn they did.

He thanked her, wondering how he would transfer the mummy without damaging it. Still, he didn't try to persuade her to help even that much. He could tell that she meant that this was as far as she was willing to go.

The premature darkness deepened as he dragged the stone boat across the road and uphill to the Valentine house. Distant thunder rolled across the valley.

Counterweight, he told himself as he shifted the log. He backed the stone boat toward the step. Tracy had known what she was talking about, because now the hitch end rested downward on the slope below the granite. All he had to do was maneuver the mummy.

But as it slid off the gate, it tipped backward. It looked hideous that way, clutching itself like a creature shrinking in fright. Still, once it lay on the stone boat, the lower center of gravity made it easier to haul.

But where to go? Not the shed with its warehouse load of antique fixtures that Eddie Shoop's Internet customers might soon be coming to look over.

Once again Duncan turned to the stinking chicken house with its surrounding fortress of briars.

He had no idea how long he spent tugging and resting and tugging some more. Finally he picked up the log and used it like a battering ram until the door crashed in. By the time he'd dragged the stone boat under cover and dumped off its burden, he could hear great, slow raindrops spatter on the sheet-metal roof of the chicken house.

Barely in time, he thought, righting the mummy and propping it up with the log so that its sightless eyes faced the open doorway.

Denny's car slowed beside Duncan and stopped.
Was Denny back with Roz?

"I'm already wet," Duncan warned. He was just returning to the road from the Mattos machine shed, where he'd left the stone boat.

"Get in," Denny said to him. "I'm going to your house."

Neither of them spoke again. Minutes later they were running for the door, which Roz opened for them. She told Duncan their parents wouldn't be home until after the meeting. He'd find leftovers in the fridge for his supper.

"You're going out?" he asked, omitting the rest of the question about its being a school night. So much for the breakup, he thought.

"We'll be back early," she told him before taking off with Denny.

Just as well, thought Duncan. He welcomed this time alone. He would do something mindless for a while before tackling the Civil War.

He foraged in the kitchen, where he opened a full bag of chips and then pried two frozen hot dogs from a started package. By the time they were nuked, he had mounds of ketchup and relish ready on a plate, which he carried into the living room. He turned on the television, but the reception, never adequate, was especially crummy. It was as good as a barometer, though, for announcing a storm.

He put on a video, a movie he'd never heard of that Roz must have rented. It was a stupid tearjerker that seemed to go on forever, but he kept watching just to see how it came out. It appeared to be winding down to its soppy ending when the telephone rang.

Tracy said, "Something's the matter with the Chicken Lady."

"What do you mean?" Duncan asked.

"She called. She says the dog's all worked up and someone's after the chickens."

"There aren't any chickens," Duncan said.

"I know that," Tracy told him. "She sounded really wacko."

Duncan thought a moment. "Can you go check on her?" he asked.

"No," Tracy said. "No way."

"You're the one she called," Duncan said.

"Not me. She thought I was Mom. She was all mixed up."

"I think it should be an adult," he said.

"Like Uncle Mace?" Tracy demanded. "I don't think so. Not after the beer he's downed."

"What about your grandfather?" asked Duncan.

"It's pouring out. He's already in bed."

Duncan wanted to say that Astrid wasn't his responsibility, but all he could manage was one last feeble plea for someone else to take over. "If your uncle isn't, you know, too drunk, wouldn't he be more effective? I mean, whether or not she actually heard someone outside, she'd feel better because she knows no one would mess with him."

"I'm not sure," Tracy replied. "Mace, he's, like, unpredictable. I can ask him, though."

"Thanks, Tracy," Duncan said to her.

After hanging up, he carried his plate to the kitchen sink and rinsed it. Then he got his foul-weather jacket out of the closet, just in case Mace Mattos refused to go over to Astrid's house. Any minute now he expected Tracy to call back to tell him her uncle was on his way. Or wasn't. But the phone didn't ring again. He figured he'd better not waste time if there really was a problem, so he took off into the wet night.

The wind had risen since he'd come home. It blew gusts of rain at his face, forcing him to bend forward. Still, he could see the roadside brighten for seconds at a time, the lightning diffuse and almost benign. It made the thunder that followed each flash all the more startling, as if it were driven by a mighty rage. Probably by now Mo would be freaking out.

Just as Duncan reached Astrid's house, he caught a glimpse of someone hurrying up her driveway. So instead of going to the front door, he ran after the person. "Mace?" he called. "Mace Mattos?"

The person paused, shouted something, and kept going. A male voice. But was it Mace? Duncan kept losing him and finding him again until he realized that the man wasn't aiming for the shed. He was heading straight for the chicken house, of all places.

All at once Duncan could see him clearly against a background of sparks and white smoke. "Wait!" Duncan called. The man seemed to be flinging himself toward the flames that crept up the lopsided walls of the wooden structure.

Duncan caught up with Mace Mattos as he stood before the chicken house, his face twisted with horror, his skin, including his baldness, a ghastly orange.

"No, no, no," Mace Mattos moaned, as Duncan grabbed his arm and dragged him back. "No. No, no, no."

Duncan followed Mace's gaze. There was the mummy, its eyes alight, small tongues of fire issuing from its mouth. It seemed to writhe, its contorted limbs released from their locked embrace. Its hair crackled, swelled, turned to smoke. Only the red-brown wrapping remained miraculously intact. Then, slowly, it fanned out in its own firestorm.

Mace lunged toward the burning figure, swiping at it, trying to stamp out the flames. When the intense heat drove him off, Duncan caught his arm again and hauled with all his strength. "Don't try to save it," he shouted at Mace.

"I didn't know," Mace babbled, "didn't know. It's a kid. Just a kid."

Was everyone around here crazy? Duncan tried to reach him with a voice of reason. "Go home," he said. "Call 911. Hurry!"

Mace shook Duncan from his arm, swung away, and ran.

Duncan ran, too. There was no telling what Mace would do. Glancing back, he saw the chicken house engulfed in flames that danced on through the dead weeds. In spite of the rain, the wind gusts prevailed, tossing the fire straight toward the shed.

He raced it, passed it, and gained the yard. As soon as he climbed over the gate he began to hear music blaring inside the house. Flinging open the door, he yelled into the kitchen through a stirring brass fanfare.

"Out! Come on, Astrid."

"I knew someone was here," she told him. "I heard a car. Someone snooping around. Trying to find a way in. Or else they already took off with my priceless—"

"Astrid!" Duncan shouted, pushing the walker up against the side of the bed. "Now." He shut off the tape player.

"Don't do that," she told him. "It keeps Mo from hearing the storm."

"Come!" Duncan insisted, his own voice huge now that the trumpet fanfare was silenced.

She didn't understand. She refused to be fussed. When he opened the front door for her, she resisted.

"It's not my kind of night," she protested. "Not Mo's either."

Duncan had to push her and her walker out of the house.

He ran back inside to dial 911, only to be told that a previous call had alerted the volunteer fire department. Yes, he was assured, the man had already informed them about a burning outbuilding on Garnet Road.

As he hung up, he thought he could hear a siren. The fire truck already? Or was it Astrid wailing in front of her house?

For a while it seemed as though the entire town meeting had reassembled on Garnet Road. First the fire truck pulled into the driveway. Next came extra volunteer firemen in their own pickups and cars. Bud and Wanda Mattos took charge of the roadside, shouting and gesturing at later arrivals to prevent their blocking access to the driveway in case backup from Brixton was needed.

Someone helped Astrid down from the granite step. But she refused to be packed away into a waiting car. "Mo!" she cried. "Mo!" It was clear that she wouldn't budge until Mo was back with her.

Duncan started around the uphill side of the house where he could watch the firefighters without getting in their way. But his father caught up with him and told him to find the damn dog so they could get Mrs. Valentine out of there.

Duncan didn't know where to begin. Word was going around that the fire was dangerously close to the house. Wouldn't Mo be terrified? Wouldn't he clear out?

Duncan left the excited crowd and took off down the road calling Mo. It could be the wrong direction, but the only time Duncan had seen Mo bolt, he was heading downhill. So down Duncan went, dodging cars and trucks. The closer he came to the main road, the more urgently he called. Tires squealed as drivers swerved and braked to avoid each other and people hurrying through the dark.

The rain had almost stopped, although thunder still muttered in the distance. Would Mo keep running from it or would he hide somewhere? On a hunch that a dog might seek shelter and maybe the comfort of other animals, Duncan turned and headed back toward the Mattos farm. Still calling Mo, he paused at the milk house and then hurried on to the barn.

At the entrance he switched on lights. Now he could move faster, cover more ground. "Mo?" he kept calling. "Here, Mo."

He heard a cow in one of the side pens stamping and then blowing through her nostrils. She might be warning Mo away. Or she might be calving. Going to check out the pen, he heard something else now, and he smelled vomit. Stopping short, he listened. Labored breathing? He peered over a partition. At first he thought this pen must be empty. Then he saw Mace Mattos face down in the bedding.

"Mace?" he said. "You all right?"

Mace gurgled something that wasn't exactly a word but which Duncan took to mean that he wanted to be left alone. So Duncan went, calling the dog more softly now, as if the search for a small dog might impinge on Mace's solitary misery.

Duncan wondered whether he should go to the farmhouse to alert Tracy or some other family member. But figuring they must still be at the fire, he continued his search along the road.

Headlights were still coming and going. In their blinding aftermath he kept spotting gray lumps on the roadside that must be Mo. Every time he dashed across and discovered that what had looked like a dead dog was a rock or tree branch, he felt dizzy with relief. He told himself to keep his head. Mo could be lying injured anywhere. He knew that if he was to find him, he would have to stay calm and focused. Yet every small mound that loomed before him was almost certainly Mo. In the grip of panic and heedless of traffic, Duncan raced over to inspect what he dreaded to confirm.

When a car stopped beside him, his first thought was that the driver had found Mo on the highway. But the driver wasn't stopping about a dog. He had stopped to get Duncan off the road before he was hit.

"I know you," the driver told Duncan. "I saw you over to Valentines'. I heard about the fire. She okay?"

Duncan recognized his voice before he could actually make out his features. It was Stan Brecher without his big truck. Duncan nodded and said, "I guess so. Her dog's missing, though."

"Get in," Stan Brecher said to him.

Duncan shook his head. "I'm looking for the dog."

A car heading downhill stopped, its headlights lighting up Stan Brecher's car.

Duncan's father called out, "Duncan! Thank God. You shouldn't be on the road like this."

A pickup truck pulled up behind Duncan's father's car.

Stan Brecher said, "I can take him up to Astrid's. You go on ahead and turn around."

Duncan rode the short distance beside Stan Brecher, who paused across from the Valentine house to let him out before driving on to find a parking spot off the road.

Duncan's mom ran to meet him. "Are you all right? Did Dad find you?"

Dazed, Duncan nodded. With all the people milling about, it took him a minute or two to locate Astrid. A chair had been brought outside for her. There she sat, leaning at an awkward angle, one arm flung across her walker as if she feared it might be snatched away. There was something in that angle, in the rigid tilt of her head, that brought to mind the lifelessness of the mummy. This was no witchy trick, this altered Astrid. Somehow he understood that.

As he walked over to her, he decided he would tell her that he'd stay home from school tomorrow to search for Mo.

She looked up at him, her eyes almost vacant. Then partial recognition seemed to come, though slowly. She said, "Stevie?"

He didn't know how to respond.

"Paul," she said. "Paul's gone. Did you know that?"

"I'm sorry," Duncan answered. "I'm really sorry."

He and his family stayed at the Valentine house until Doris showed up. By then Mom and Wanda Mattos were working out shifts for staying with Astrid. But from the moment Doris pushed through to them, she called the shots.

"Come on, then," Doris said to Astrid. "You're lucky. Your house survived."

Astrid said, "Oh, Doris, there was something I had to tell you."

"It can wait," Doris responded, helping Astrid to her feet.

"It'll have to. It's slipped my mind. Where's Mo?" She rambled on. "I wish you'd tell me what all these people are doing here. Damn. I think I wet my pants."

"Probably just the rain," Doris said to her. "Everything's wet. Say good night."

Briskly she guided Astrid to the step. Several people rushed forward to help, but Doris shook them off. She said, "Thanks. Give her a moment."

Everyone watched Astrid struggle to lift herself onto the stone. Then she turned around and started to back her way up.

Doris warded off outstretched hands.

Dragging the walker right to the edge of the step, Astrid swiveled and launched herself hard. Only there wasn't quite enough lift to clear the step, and she landed sprawling on the granite. "Made it!" she crowed in triumph, while Doris reset the walker and helped Astrid into it. At the door Astrid turned partway around and spoke to everyone standing there. She said, "Thanks for coming. I'd ask you in, but I think it's getting late."

She steered the walker across her threshold and halted. Then she turned once again. "Mo!" she called. Looking directly at Duncan she asked, "Is he in the back yard?"

"I'll go look," Duncan said.

That seemed to reassure her, because she let Doris shut the door.

By then he was staggering with exhaustion, and his parents wouldn't let him go anywhere but home. "I promised to look," he said.

"You're done," his mother told him. "Doris will look. She'll stay the night." She caught sight of Roz and Denny on the fringe of the shrinking crowd. "You, too. Home."

"Mom!" Roz said. "We're celebrating. We're back together."

"I said home," Mom replied, steering Roz in that general direction. "With us. Good night, Denny."

Still in his clothes, Duncan flopped down on his bed. He fell asleep listening to his parents downstairs blowing off steam. Mom was furious that Dad had sent Duncan to find the dog, and Dad was furious because he never imagined that Duncan would go where there was traffic instead of into the woods or some such place a dog would go. They had already made it clear that Duncan could not stay home from school tomorrow.

He woke aching in the morning. A hot shower felt good while it lasted, but after he dressed, the aches and stiffness returned. He tried to convince his mother that he was on the verge of a dire illness, but she just replied that he could hunt for the dog after school.

He left early enough to stop at the Valentine house. "Any sign of Mo?" he asked as Doris raised a warning finger to her lips and shook her head.

In the kitchen Astrid in her hospital bed whimpered, "Mo? Mo, Mo."

"He'll be back," Duncan said, going to her. "I'll bring him home. He was just waiting for the crowd to go away."

Half of Astrid's mouth stretched in a lopsided smile. "Drew a big crowd, did we?"

He nodded.

"Nothing like a swinging gig!" All at once her eye twitched. "You!" she drawled. "You're the trumpet kid. Right?"

"Yes," he replied. Did she mean him or someone else she called Stevie? He turned on the tape she had been playing last night to drown out the fearsome thunder and inspire courage in her cowering dog. Then he had to go. The clear, triumphant notes followed him almost to the highway.

Tracy said, "Here's the bus. You nearly missed it."

He wanted to ask about her uncle Mace. But once they stepped inside the bus, they stuck to their habit of taking separate seats. Maybe after school. He might even talk her into helping him look for Mo.

It turned out that everyone on the bus knew about the fire. Both Tracy and Duncan were plied with questions. Going into school they were mobbed. Tracy rose to this celebrity status, speaking as an instant expert on fires and other disasters and as a reliable observer of the brave and the cowardly on hand for the occasion.

Duncan didn't know how to handle the attention. He kept his answers brief and flat. At lunch kids surrounded him. There was a rumor about Mace Mattos getting himself burned. Who had saved him from the flames? Did Old Lady Valentine really pee on her front steps? Did they catch the guy who shot her dog?

All Duncan could do was to tell them no, no, and no. He tried to explain that a lot of the time he hadn't actually been there.

But they kept after him until he was so fed up he didn't want to speak to anyone, not now, not later. No, not even to Tracy after school.

After stepping down from the bus, Duncan started up the road at a brisk pace without looking back.

But Tracy, turned on by her day of celebrity treatment, charged after him. Even before she caught up, she called to him. "Did you know my uncle freaked out big-time?"

Duncan slowed. "I was going to tell someone."

"Tell them what?" she asked as she reached his side.

"You know. That he got all weird. He threw up, too."

Tracy said, "Sometimes he can be ... scary."

"Scary how?" Duncan asked.

Tracy said, "It's like sometimes he doesn't know us. Doesn't know where he is. Mom guesses he's in Vietnam. My father says Uncle Mace must be in hell. Grandpa says Vietnam and hell are all the same for Uncle Mace. See, Dad's a lot younger. He was just a kid back then, so all he knows about that war is what he's seen on the tube."

"Your uncle never talks about it?"

Tracy shook her head. "Only when he's drunk or high or both. Then what he says never makes sense."

Duncan wondered if he could unscramble the few words Mace Mattos had spoken last night. But they were too fragmented. Anyway, it didn't really matter now. He needed to concentrate on finding Mo.

He didn't ask Tracy to help him. He just said, "See you," as she turned in at the farm. He supposed he ought to check on Astrid in case someone had already found the dog and called her. First, though, he'd make a quick daylight sweep around the house.

Starting at the driveway, which was scored with wheel tracks, he made his way to the back. He was stunned at how altered everything was. The collapsed chicken house was reduced to a few corrugated strips of buckled roof arching over blackened rubble. The piercing stench from beneath bore an overlay of sweetness that hinted at the familiar aroma of wood smoke. The long shed still stood, but the wall across from the chicken house was gutted, the roof steeply pitched where supports had given way.

He knew enough to keep clear of the actual burn area, but he came close enough to feel heat. Maybe something still smoldered deep inside the derelict building.

He called Mo, waited, and called again. A crow flying overhead cawed, and from the woods other crows squawked and flapped. The approaching crow dropped to a branch. He supposed he should check out the place in the woods where the crows had gathered. They could be tearing at some small prey. But he dreaded discovering that the prey was Mo.

Turning away from the woods, he went through the fenced yard to the back door to see Astrid before resuming his search. As soon as he was inside he could tell that the house was deserted. He found a scribbled note Doris Beasley had left for him on the Hoosier cabinet. It read: "Astrid gone to hospital—call later."

He stood for a moment staring at the brief message, as if a thorough rereading might yield more information. Then he let himself out the front door.

Late that afternoon, while he was still outside looking for Mo,

Tracy came to find him and filled him in on what had happened with Astrid. Doris had called in sick at her job and was staying at the house to keep an eye on Astrid. She was trying to deal with the living room mess while Astrid listened to her music. Then when Astrid fell asleep, Doris turned off the tape and went back to the cleanup. But after a while she had a feeling something was wrong. She tried to wake up Astrid, who couldn't be roused. That was when Doris called the doctor and then Wanda, who came right over and waited with her until the ambulance arrived.

"What's wrong with Astrid?" Duncan asked.

Tracy said, "My mom thinks it's another stroke. Doris is at the hospital. I guess she'll call when they know more."

Duncan said, "I can't find Mo. I've looked everywhere."

"Give it up," Tracy told him. "If he wasn't run over, he'll be coyote prey."

Thanks a lot, Duncan thought, but all he said was, "If he's just hurt somewhere, he might hear me calling him."

"And do what?" Tracy asked. "Whine just loud enough to let you know where he is? You must watch a lot of Disney movies."

Duncan was too discouraged to reply.

Tracy said, "Anyway, I thought you couldn't stand the little mop with a mouth."

He turned away, back to the woods. He would take the upland road as far as the rock face. After that he'd call it a day.

It was a stroke. Everyone said the stress of the fire had tipped Astrid over the edge.

"You'd think the nephew would come," Doris said to Duncan's parents. She was staying at Astrid's house over the weekend in case the dog showed up.

"It's not like he hasn't put his own affairs on hold to be here a lot," Dad remarked.

"That's true," Mom agreed. "He's been super attentive to his aunt."

Doris pressed her lips together and managed not to reply.

Duncan considered bringing the bags of carved bones back to Astrid's. But he wasn't sure they should be left in her house if no one was going to be there during the week. So he shoved them to the back of the downstairs closet. They'd be safe there with the winter boots until Astrid was well enough to decide what to do with them.

Saturday afternoon Curt Barrington, Chiswick's constable, stopped by to talk with the Veerick family. Roz was off with Denny. Dad was working in Brixton. So Mom and Duncan sat down with Curt in the kitchen while she made coffee.

"I've been getting an earful from Doris," he told Mom. "It's a pity she and Astrid fell out like that. Doris blames it on the nephew, but I suppose you know all about it."

Mom said, "Yes. I think it happened because Astrid hates

being helpless. Since Doris was the one who helped most, Astrid kind of took out her frustration on her."

Curt nodded. "Astrid's never been that easy to get along with."

Duncan couldn't help wondering whether Curt's remark was based on hearsay or direct experience. He was a big, gentle man with a quiet way of speaking. It was hard to picture him dealing with Astrid in one of her stubborn moods.

Mom said, "Any news about her?"

Curt shook his head. "No news is good news, I hope. But that's not why I'm here. See, Wanda and Bud think the fire may have been started."

"You mean deliberately?" Mom gasped. "Good heavens!"

"Well, there was spread lightning, all right," he said, "but no one recalls any hits close to ground. And then there's that call Astrid made just before the fire. Told the Mattos girl someone was out back."

"But going after her chickens," Duncan blurted. "She doesn't have any."

Curt Barrington tuned to Duncan. "I know. Still, afterward she kept insisting she'd heard someone behind her house. Anyhow, it won't hurt to look into it."

"Can you tell about the fire?" Mom asked him.

"Andy Keezer is coming over from Brixton to look at the site. He's a state fire marshal. Meanwhile, I just thought I'd ask around in case any of you neighbors saw or heard anything."

Duncan said, "Astrid was afraid of being robbed."

"She told you that?"

Duncan nodded. "She even made me move stuff out of the house." Thinking of the stone sculptures, he exclaimed, "Oh!"

"Oh, what?" Curt asked.

"Well, I took her stone things to the chicken house."

"What stone things?" Mom asked.

"Eskimo carvings."

Curt Barrington rose from his chair. "You took them to the chicken house? Why?"

"Well, to hide them," Duncan told him. Then he added, "It stank. There were brambles and nettles and stuff. No one would look there for valuable—you know, art."

Curt thought a moment, gulped down the rest of his coffee, and started for the door. Then, turning back, he asked, "When you went over that night, did you see anyone at all? Did you hear a car or truck?"

Duncan shook his head. "Only Mace Mattos. Tracy sent him to look around."

Curt Barrington said, "Well, I can't get anything out of him."

Duncan said, "He freaked out. Tracy says fires give him bad memories."

Curt Barrington sighed. "We all know about Mace."

"I'm afraid we're not much help either," Mom said.

"Well, it'll probably amount to nothing. Thanks for the coffee, Natalie. Thanks, Duncan. We'll let you all know what, if anything, Andy Keezer comes up with."

Duncan followed him to the door. "What if someone finds her dog?" he asked. "Do you think they'll tell you?"

"People are supposed to report strays. But if it's dead, well ..." The constable didn't finish.

Duncan said, "Could you tell me if you hear anything about him?"

Curt Barrington nodded. "You bet. Astrid's lucky to have a neighbor like you."

After he was gone Mom sat awhile absently sipping her coffee. When Duncan started up the stairs, she said, "I wish you'd told us about Astrid's fear. I wish we'd known. She must have felt so isolated."

He said, "Eddie Shoop knew. He warned her to be careful. Because people could find her place. People interested in what she had. She was getting seriously scared."

Mom nodded. Then she said, "Curt's right. She was lucky to have you. I'm afraid the rest of us let her down."

Duncan continued on up the stairs. All he wanted now was to zone out. He'd had enough.

The vacation week ahead spread before him, a limitless horizon. He and Neil Gortler would hang out. They'd invent games and special projects for Neil's younger brother and sisters. Besides, they had this cool trampoline. Of course he and Neil would set aside one day for themselves to go climbing. A whole week just doing what he liked.

When Astrid recovered and came home again, he told himself, he would try to make up for getting her mummy burned. Not only would he help out as before, but he'd lose the attitude. Never again would he dismiss her worries and suspicions, no matter how loony they sounded.

What Andy Keezer found outside the chicken house confirmed Wanda's and Bud's suspicions. By early in the week everyone in Chiswick must have heard that stones wrapped in gasoline-soaked rags had been hurled inside the chicken house. One had fallen short.

"The puzzle is why anyone would do such a thing," Curt Barrington said to Duncan's parents. "Oh, and by the way, a call came in. Tom Lassiter and his girlfriend found a small gray dog, no license. You know where they live, just past the pond? Give them a call before you go see it."

Dad nodded. "Good. We'll check it out."

"Can we go now?" Duncan asked. Mo had to be hungry and confused, maybe still terrified. If he was injured, he'd need a vet.

"After we hear whatever else Curt has to tell us," said Duncan's father.

"Well, that's about it so far. Andy's sifting through the rubble now. Oh, yes, and the nephew showed up. He'd stopped at the hospital. I guess he's some riled. He's already managed to blast Doris for straightening up the house. Meddling, he called it. Claims he can't find stuff he needs, records he was seeing to for Astrid."

"Poor, good Doris," Mom said. "How did she take it?"

"Got in her car and drove away." Curt shook his head. "I feel bad for both of them."

—

As soon as Curt had left, Duncan's father called Tom Lassiter. Then he drove Duncan to see the dog. On the way he said, "They've become attached to it. They asked about keeping it."

"Well, they can't," Duncan said. "Not if it's Mo."

"Someone has to take care of it. They took it in."

When they got to Tom Lassiter's, Duncan was out of the car and at the front door before his father was halfway to the house.

Tom and Emmy led Duncan and his father into their spotless kitchen. The little dog that rose from the folded blanket on the floor was almost unrecognizable, but not in the way Duncan expected. This Mo was bathed and groomed and so self-possessed that even his greeting was muted. He looked at Duncan, wagged his tail, and then sauntered over to the two dishes neatly arranged for him on a towel. He lapped a little water, sniffed, and discovered one leftover kibble beside the other dish. Crunching with evident satisfaction and still amiably wagging his tail, he approached Tom and Emmy and the Veericks, looked up at them, and sat down.

Duncan couldn't believe this transformation. The appearance, yes. But Mo's manner of greeting, without frenzied circles and yips, how could this be? "Mo?" he said tentatively. "Mo, come!"

The dog got up and came to him.

"Well?" said Dad.

Duncan didn't speak. What if this was a look-alike? But that was impossible. "When did you find him?" he asked.

"He found us," Emmy told him. "The night of the storm. We looked for a name on his collar. Then we called him Scamp and he came inside."

"He was a mess," Tom said. "So we cleaned him up. We fed him chicken soup and bread. Then we got dog food."

Duncan nodded. It was Mo, all right. And he didn't look too eager to leave this cushy new home.

Duncan's father said, "If you want to keep him for now, I'm sure that would be fine with Astrid's nephew. No one knows how long it will be before she can come home."

Emmy said, "We'd be happy to take care of him. Especially if there's a chance that it's for good."

Duncan said, "But Astrid was so worried. We should bring Mo to her. Seeing him might be just what she needs." Even as he spoke, Duncan could hear Tracy sneering at this sentimental scenario.

Emmy said, "Of course. We'll help work out visits whenever you want."

Duncan and his father left the new and improved Mo there for the time being. Dad said, "I'll call Doris Beasley. She'll want to know that the dog is safe."

"I'll tell Eddie," Duncan said. "I have to talk to him anyway." About the bones, Duncan thought, uncertain whether he still needed to keep the mummy's existence a secret. After all, it was actually nonexistent now. Except that Astrid didn't know this yet.

Duncan's dad dropped him off in front of the Valentine house. Two cars were in the driveway, another car and a truck parked on the road. Eddie Shoop might be out back with people investigating the fire. Duncan hoped not. No one but Doris and Eddie would appreciate what Mo meant to Astrid.

As Duncan unlocked the front door, ready to burst into the house, he heard Eddie's voice berating someone. Was he talking on the phone? He sounded just the way Curt Barrington had described him: riled.

Duncan stopped, the door ajar, and waited for Eddie to finish.

"It had to be a lightning strike," Eddie was saying. "I told you."

Someone spoke. "It was. There was lightning. Like you said."

"They're investigating," Eddie snapped, his voice low and intense.

"It won't amount to anything. You'll see. Anyway, nothing major was lost. You'll be able to pick up from here, no problem." But the speaker sounded worried, as if some deal hadn't quite panned out.

"Well …" Eddie fell silent.

There was a sigh, no more words.

When Duncan heard someone get up and start walking toward the hall, he thought he'd better announce himself. So he slammed the door and called, "Eddie?"

"What?" Eddie yelled, striding out of the living room behind Stan Brecher.

"I'll be off, then," said Stan. Nodding at Duncan as he stepped past him, he opened the door just wide enough to squeeze out.

"Good news!" Duncan said to Eddie. "Mo's been found. He's fine."

"Oh," said Eddie. "Mo. Right. He's okay?"

Duncan nodded. "I've just been to see him. I thought you'd want to know right away. In case you want to take him to Astrid," Duncan finished.

Eddie said, "Astrid's in pretty poor shape. She won't know if Mo's there."

Duncan had expected more of a reaction. "I thought you'd be glad," he said.

Eddie ran his hand through his hair. He looked drawn, pre-occupied. "I am. Of course I am. I'm just coming to terms with everything. The fire. It was … The way it spread, it could have reached the house." He drew a breath. "The dog, yes. I know he means the world to her."

"Later then, when she's better," Duncan said.

Eddie nodded. "That's right. When she's better. Thanks, Duncan. I appreciate you stopping by."

Sensing that he was being dismissed, Duncan turned to leave. Out on the road he considered looking at whatever was going on in back. But they probably wouldn't let him near enough to see anything. Had they found the stone sculptures in the nesting boxes? Only there couldn't be any nesting boxes left, so the stones would be somewhere on the bottom of all the burned stuff.

He didn't go back to see. Eddie wanted him gone, just the way he'd seemed to want Stan Brecher gone. So Duncan walked on up the road.

He hadn't gotten around to mentioning the carved bones either. Maybe holding back wasn't such a bad idea. It still troubled Duncan that Astrid had wanted the bones hidden away. Hidden from Eddie. It couldn't hurt to wait until she was well enough to speak her mind.

While he was thinking about them, as soon as he got home he stopped to retrieve the carved owl from one of the paper bags at the back of the coat closet. He took it up to his room, looked around, and decided to try hanging it on his wall. Maybe when Astrid came home he could do something like that for her so that she could enjoy some of her things without risk of their being chewed.

For the time being, though, until he could find a hook or nail, he stuck the owl on his collection shelf. The glass doorknob was still there, too. He picked it up and took it down to the coat closet to keep with the bones that would eventually go back to the Valentine house.

There was nothing else that needed doing. Mo was safe. So were the bones. He could relax for a while and take things as they came.

By the middle of the following week the fire had become old news. Duncan, returning to his pre-Astrid schedule, felt as if he'd arrived home from a distant land. Extra trumpet lessons and rehearsals put him sort of back on track. The music for "When the Saints Go Marching In" that Mr. Simon came up with nearly made it into the band program. Duncan didn't care one way or another so long as he could work on the piece on his own. He had time for that, too, as well as for other things.

Eddie Shoop went away and came back. No one paid much attention to him except to inquire about Astrid, whose condition improved in some ways and declined in others.

On Friday morning Curt Barrington showed up in school and called Duncan into the principal's outer office, where he asked questions he'd already asked. Then he added a few more, mostly about Mace Mattos.

After school Tracy said, "Mr. Barrington thinks Uncle Mace might have started the fire. He asked me about it."

"Me too," Duncan said.

They stopped on the road while they talked.

"Wasn't the hen house burning when you got there?"

"Yes."

"And you didn't see anyone else?"

"Just your uncle. I told Curt Barrington."

"And I told him Uncle Mace went there because I asked him to check out the place after Mrs. Valentine called. Dad says when Mr. Barrington asked Uncle Mace about it, he said it was his fault. He thought it was about a different fire, about torching some enemy house that turned out to have no one but a child in it. I hope the chief gets how mixed up Uncle Mace can be."

Duncan said, "Just because your uncle thinks it was his fault doesn't mean it was. Can't your dad explain that to Curt Barrington?"

"He tried," Tracy told him. "It's weird, isn't it, Mrs. Valentine knowing that something was going on out there. Funny she didn't call you," she added.

"You were closer," Duncan replied.

Tracy scowled, shrugged, and walked on.

He took his time going home. Now that he was released from the Valentine house, what he relished most was time, time to waste or time to pack up climbing gear. He would call Neil to settle on their Saturday departure. He was growing out of his climbing shoes. Neil, whose feet were much bigger, was saving an old pair for him. It might not be a bad idea to try them out. Duncan's thoughts wandered, lazed, recalled the goal he and Neil had set for themselves. Stark Bluff. A serious climb. Their parents didn't need to know that. The weekend opened up before him, filling him with a sense of well-being.

Roz came home stormy again, this time railing at someone named Cindy. Duncan ducked away, closing himself into his room. Later he went down to the kitchen to see what he could find for tomorrow's trek. He wanted to keep his backpack light, but he knew he'd work up a thirst. He settled for a protein bar, almonds, and two bottles of water. Neil usually brought rope and chocolate enough for them both. Duncan was back upstairs when his parents came home.

They called up to him and to Roz. He answered, but his sister could barely be heard. She didn't join them for supper either, although she appeared in the kitchen briefly to forage in the refrigerator on her own. Mom shrugged. Dad tried being extra loving and concerned. He was rebuffed. Mom shrugged again. Duncan stared at the kitchen table.

He sat awhile watching an old movie with his parents, but he couldn't stop yawning. Finally he got up and dragged himself to bed.

Saturday dawned slightly overcast with a smear of light on the eastern horizon.

"Give it an hour or two," said Neil when they met on the upland road. "It'll clear."

Duncan said, "Don't bet on it. And don't wish for it either, or we'll be cooked."

They set off full of energy, vying with each other, as usual, for the first sighting of any of the less common animals that inhabited the woods. Last fall they'd spied a fisher in a tree, so they still glanced upward as well as into the undergrowth along their path.

By the time they reached Stark Bluff the sun had broken through the cloud cover, bringing a hint of haze and heat. They peeled off jackets and sneakers and then stretched out for a moment before putting on their harnesses and climbing shoes.

"Turkey vulture!" Neil declared, pointing skyward.

"Two of them," said Duncan as a second bird circled and dipped above the first.

"Something killed or just born?" Neil suggested as more turkey vultures appeared and then dropped below the treeline.

Duncan sat up. "Maybe we should listen first," he said.

Neil nodded, but he rose to his feet, ready to check out whatever it was that attracted the scavengers.

Nodding in agreement, they put their sneakers back on and left their jackets and climbing gear at the base of the bluff. But one snapping twig was enough to give them away. They never even saw the ravenous birds until they had taken flight, and then they could barely be spotted overhead. The boys searched the area from which the turkey vultures had risen, but whatever prey had drawn them had either escaped or been consumed.

Neither of them minded the delay. They had all day. Back at the base of the bluff Duncan tried on Neil's outgrown climbing shoes, which almost fit. Then they started up the familiar side. It was challenging enough for the first ascent of the season. Duncan made one bad slip, his left hand raking the granite, skin and nails tearing before the rope caught his fall. After that they regrouped, taking their time and the better part of the morning to reach the summit. Once there, they stayed awhile, surveying the near slopes and distant mountains.

"Look!" Neil whispered, pointing to something dark that moved between the trees below them.

Duncan followed Neil's gaze. After a moment a black bear ambled into a small clearing. She was followed by two cubs.

The top of Stark Bluff was perfect for bear watching because the boys didn't have to worry about being detected. They didn't speak. They simply watched until the sow and her cubs had merged with the tree shadows and disappeared.

Duncan's father was standing near his car. "There
he is!" he called toward the house. "He's just coming now."

Curt Barrington and another man appeared in the doorway. They waited for Duncan to draw near before they spoke.

"We need to talk," Curt Barrington finally said.

Craving something cold and wet, Duncan headed for the kitchen.

"In here," said Curt Barrington, indicating the living room.

"I just want to get a drink," Duncan explained.

"I'll bring it to you," his mother said. "These ... We've been waiting for you." She sounded strange, though whether cross or worried, Duncan couldn't tell.

Duncan was introduced to a man and a woman, Officers Keezer and Firth, both from Brixton, as far as Duncan could tell.

"There have been developments," Curt Barrington said to Duncan. He sounded different, more official. "We've just informed your parents about them."

Duncan nodded. He waited. Then his mother appeared with a glass of orange juice, which he quickly drained. He waited some more.

Curt Barrington said, "You know that we've examined the fire scene."

Duncan nodded again, wondering if he should speak up for Mace Mattos.

"Bone fragments were collected from the site," Curt Barrington continued. "Andy—Officer Keezer suspected they were human bones, but we couldn't be sure until they were analyzed in the state forensics lab. Do you understand what I'm saying, Duncan?"

Duncan nodded again. He said, "You didn't need to send them to a lab. If you'd—"

Duncan's mother said, "They didn't want anyone to know until they could get a positive confirmation."

"But I know what they are," Duncan said.

"You knew about the human remains?" Curt Barrington demanded.

"Yes. They *are* human," Duncan tried to explain, "but not what you think. Or what Mace Mattos thought. He couldn't've started the fire because—"

"Never mind Mace," Officer Keezer interrupted. "Tell us what you know. What you should have told Curt from the outset."

His indignation confused Duncan, who thought he'd answered every question so far. Curt Barrington drew his chair closer to Duncan. "Just tell us what you know," he said.

Duncan nodded. "What burned up in that fire was a mummy. A mummy from Peru. I didn't think there was anything left, because I saw it on fire. That was when Mace saw it. He thinks it's his fault because of something that happened in Vietnam a long time ago. Tracy's family says it's a kind of flashback."

"Let's stick to the point," Curt Barrington said quietly. "How do you know it was a mummy?"

"They had this one left from years ago. Astrid didn't want

anyone to know. Not even Eddie Shoop, because he found out about the ones they'd had before and said it was against the law to import them and sell them. But Astrid said it was one of her treasures, so she made me get it out of the house. She wanted it in the Mattos barn, but Tracy wouldn't help, so I put it in the chicken house. I never thought there'd be a fire. Astrid said it was worth ..." Was this a betrayal now? Should he say what the previous one sold for? "They're very valuable," he finished.

Curt Barrington pulled back and turned to look at Officer Keezer.

For a moment no one spoke. Then Duncan's mother said, "It doesn't make sense. Who would burn it?" When no one replied, she went on. "No one we know would do such a thing."

Curt Barrington said to Duncan, "Are you sure Astrid wanted to hide the mummy from her nephew? Did she tell you that?"

Duncan nodded. "She was really insistent about it, too. She'll probably tell you herself. I mean, after she finds out you know about it now. She said Eddie was too law-abiding, that he'd ..." Duncan hesitated.

"That he'd what?" Officer Keezer prompted.

"You know, keep her from selling it. She thought she had a buyer, but I'm not sure about that. Anyway, she made me get it out of the house before Eddie came back. I didn't know what to do with it. She's going to be really upset when she finds out."

Officer Keezer said, "I think we need to talk with Mr. Shoop again." He stood up.

Curt Barrington said to Duncan, "I want to be sure you've told us all you know. Think about it." He turned to the woman. "How about you, Lois? Anything you want to add?"

Then the woman officer spoke up. "Maybe something will

come to you later, Duncan. Memory can play tricks on us. Just keep your mind open. Okay?"

Duncan said, "There were other treasures in the chicken house. Eskimo carvings. Astrid calls them sculptures. I was supposed to bury them in a secret place so they wouldn't be stolen. I didn't have time." He faltered. "Is that what you wanted to know?"

Curt Barrington nodded. "Some have been recovered. A few are still intact. Eddie Shoop says the ruined ones are a serious loss."

Duncan realized they were all looking at him. Because he had left the sculptures in harm's way? Did that make him responsible for that serious loss?

His parents followed the three officers to the front door. Duncan found it hard to summon the strength just to stand. All his energy seemed to have been drained, though not by the miles he had tramped through the woods or by scaling Stark Bluff. When his parents returned to the living room, they looked tense.

He said, "I wish they'd talk to Astrid."

Mom said, "She's been moved from the hospital."

"Good!" Duncan exclaimed. "When do you think she'll be able to speak for herself? She can tell them everything."

Mom shook her head. "She was moved because she's not getting better."

"I bet she would be if they brought Mo to see her."

Mom drew a long breath. "Duncan, you need to understand. This stroke isn't like the last one. They don't expect her to recover. Which might be a blessing," she added when Duncan failed to respond. "They think she'd be severely impaired if she lived."

Duncan let this information sink in. Then, stubbornly, he said, "Even so, it's not fair to keep Mo from her."

"That's not up to us," Dad told him.

"Why is it up to us to help her and take care of her dog," Duncan blurted, "and then suddenly not up to us about something that matters to her more than anything else?"

Dad sighed. "Because of her condition. And because of the fire," he added. Then, on a note of irritation, he said, "It would have been helpful if you'd told us about that mummy in the first place." He strode out of the living room.

"Why is he mad at me?" Duncan asked his mother.

Mom said, "He's worried. He's embarrassed. Duncan, this is a police investigation."

"I know that. Do you think I don't know that?"

"Well, there are things you could explain that you haven't," she told him.

"Like what?" he shouted.

Her voice dropped so low he barely heard her say, "Like more than a hundred dollars in your back pocket. I go through pockets before I load the washing machine. Where did all that money come from?"

"I didn't even count it." He shook his head, amazed. "Tracy got thirty. She asked what I got, but we had to keep moving, and I didn't look."

His mother said, "You have to be careful. Careful, Duncan."

He was exhausted now. Being careful made no sense. Astrid being moved somewhere and unable to speak made no sense. Unless they were wrong about her. Astrid could still surprise everyone and recover. Even if it took longer than last time, she could wake up eventually and realize that he hadn't walked out on her. Otherwise how would she ever know he'd kept his promise and found Mo?

Duncan's mother said, "Duncan? Did you hear me? Do you understand?"

He started to shake his head. But he could tell from her expression it was the wrong response, so he nodded instead.

He had a feeling something more was required, something reassuring. He felt the torn nails on his left hand dig into his palm. He tried to unclench his fists, but his fingers still seemed to be clawing at the rock face, reaching for a crevice that could hold him.

He said, "There was a bear with twin cubs. We saw them from the bluff."

If only he could revive that long, soundless moment when the mother bear and her cubs had padded out from the tree shadows, unsuspecting, unafraid.

On Sunday morning Duncan decided to try one more time to convince Eddie Shoop to bring Mo to Astrid. He found Eddie seated in the kitchen beside the empty hospital bed with a mug of coffee nestled in the pillow, the laptop perched on the stripped mattress.

Eddie said, "I appreciate what you want. I really do. But the nursing home wouldn't allow it. Astrid's not the only patient in the room. Besides, she doesn't know where she is. She doesn't respond."

"That's just it," Duncan insisted. "It might be different if she felt Mo next to her."

Eddie stretched his arms high above his head and then let them drop to his knees. He spoke through a yawn. "Thanks, Duncan. I know you want to help."

Duncan was on his way out when Eddie asked, "So whose idea was it to put the sculptures in the chicken house?"

"Astrid wanted me to bury them," Duncan said. "The chicken house was just temporary."

"I'll say," Eddie muttered. Then he added, "No. Sorry. You were doing your best for her. And we both know that once she gets an idea in her head, she won't be budged. I hear you got her out of the house when the fire was spreading. That's what matters. It's bad enough that she had the stroke. It's worse to think how close she came to being trapped in a burning house."

Duncan's thoughts raced backward through that afternoon and night. He had dealt with Astrid's stubbornness and bullying. It was her paranoia that seemed so ugly, so impossible to accept. Like her not trusting Tracy when she had sent him to the refrigerator for the wad of bills. He said, "I think she paid me too much. She was in a hurry, so she sort of shoved some money at me."

"Don't worry about it," Eddie told him. "I'm sure you earned it."

Encouraged by his kindness, Duncan asked him who he thought had started the fire.

"I wouldn't point a finger at anyone," Eddie answered. "I'm the stranger around here. Leave it to the authorities."

"They thought Mace Mattos might've done it," Duncan said. "They were wrong. Anyway, why would he? Why would anyone?"

"Good question," Eddie replied. "It could've been a stupid prank. No harm meant."

Duncan left the Valentine house feeling relieved because the nephew didn't blame him for the mummy fiasco. But he felt hopeless about getting Mo to Astrid.

Instead of going home, he headed down to the Mattos farm to let Tracy know that the police hadn't seemed that concerned about her uncle Mace anymore. It also occurred to him that he had never told her what he'd done with the mummy. He'd fill her in on it now.

Before he could start telling her any of this, she burst out in a tirade. "You're still talking to Mr. Barrington? You ought to know how pissed off my folks are. Even Grandpa. My dad and Curt Barrington are old friends, but that didn't stop Mr. Barrington from turning on Uncle Mace when he was looking for someone to blame. The way Mr. Barrington sees it, whoever started the fire as good as killed a person."

"It's over," Duncan told her. "Or almost. See, they found human bones in the chicken house and thought it was a murder. Then I explained about the mummy. So now it's only a fire to investigate, and I told them your uncle couldn't've done it."

For an instant Tracy seemed struck dumb. Then she said, "I was talking about Astrid Valentine. She's the victim, and now they say she might not get better." She paused. "So the mummy was there? Uncle Mace saw it on fire? He needs to know that."

"At least the police know. That's what I came to tell you. They asked me all kinds of questions I didn't get. I think they're looking for something else, maybe a motive for starting the fire."

Tracy said, "Well, it's none of our business anymore."

Duncan said, "I feel bad, though. I mean, if I hadn't put the mummy in the chicken house, it wouldn't've been destroyed."

"I bet the nephew's ripped about that," she said.

Duncan shook his head. "Not really. He's been okay with me. He says what bothers him is how close the fire came to the house and Astrid."

"You be careful," Tracy told him.

"That's what my mother says," Duncan answered. "Careful of what?"

She shrugged. "I don't know. Somebody probably won't mind who gets blamed as long as it isn't him. Unless," she added, "the whole thing is dropped now that they know about the mummy. Then you and Uncle Mace are both out of it. Be glad, but careful."

Glad? thought Duncan as he walked slowly home. It seemed indecent to be glad if Astrid was doing so badly.

When Duncan saw cars in front of his house again, he nearly turned around and went back to the Mattos farm. But he was working out a plan now. So he entered his house determined to ask his mother to arrange a brief bedside visit for him and Mo.

The first thing he noticed when he went inside was how stunned his parents looked. Roz, too. She sat hunched on the footstool like a frightened child.

"Where have you been?" his father demanded. "You keep going off."

Unnerved, Duncan said, "Nowhere. I mean, well, at the Valentine house. At the farm with Tracy. Why?"

"We were looking for you," Curt Barrington said.

Only then did Duncan notice the two bags of carved bones. The owl vertebra he'd left in his room was perched on top of one of the bags.

"Hey," he said, "those are Astrid's treasures." He reached for the owl and then let his hand drop to his side. How could he claim it now? Only Astrid could back him up, and she was silenced, her gift-giving erased.

Curt Barrington said, "Eddie Shoop was sure they had to be close by."

Duncan started to explain why the bones were here. But when it became clear that no one believed him, he fell silent.

"What about this?" Curt Barrington asked, holding out something else.

Duncan leaned forward to see what was in the constable's hand. It was the faceted glass doorknob.

"Oh, that," Duncan said. "It's nothing. I forgot it was here. Then I put it with the bones to take back with them."

Curt Barrington said, "Eddie Shoop's been looking for Astrid's bone carvings. He told us she'd been searching for them, too. She suspected that Doris Beasley had them. So we had to question her and look for them in her house. How do you think that made her feel, Duncan?"

"Astrid blamed Doris for anything she couldn't find," Duncan answered. "She was suspicious of anyone who contacted Eddie about the stuff he planned to sell. That's why she made me hide things."

"Were you supposed to bury the bones along with the stone sculptures?" Curt Barrington asked him.

Duncan shook his head. "She was afraid they'd be eaten. She told me to get them out of her house and bring them here. So I did."

"Don't you think you should've told us about them when we questioned you before?"

"I don't know," Duncan answered. "There were things she didn't want anyone to know about, even Eddie. I told you that. I was keeping them until she came home."

"Even though we're investigating a fire that was deliberately set? How much did you resent being her errand boy? Enough to get even with her?"

Duncan said, "Of course I minded doing all that stuff. Especially when she kept changing what she wanted. But not about the bones. That was no big deal, and they were safe here. Besides, they didn't have anything to do with the fire." Then he asked, "What will you do with them?"

"We'll hold on to them for now," Curt Barrington said. "Eventually Eddie Shoop will have them back."

Duncan felt like explaining all over again that Astrid had wanted her treasures kept from Eddie as well as Doris and everyone else.

The woman named Lois Firth asked, "Is there anything else you can tell us to help complete the picture of what happened? Take your time, Duncan. Say what's on your mind. Help us understand."

Duncan shook his head. None of them understood. Or else they didn't want to. But now he did. He fully understood that he had taken Mace Mattos' place as the person least deserving of anyone's trust.

There was nothing more to be said. All he could do was wait for them to go away.

After the interview, Duncan retreated from his father's angry accusations and his mother's panic-driven defense by shutting himself in his room, which he no longer recognized. Everything he owned, everything he had made or worn or cared about, was spread all over. It was as though the chaos in Astrid's house, like some mutant virus, had migrated up the road to invade Duncan's space. He couldn't bear to touch anything here. All the same he was trapped, reduced to waiting for any kind of distraction, even the ring of the telephone, to halt or muffle the wrangling downstairs.

When a phone call did come, Duncan left his room, eager to speak to anyone normal. As Roz answered the phone, their mother was in the midst of reminding their father of Duncan's swift response to the fire emergency.

Poised at the top of the stairs, Duncan froze. All at once it came to him that he had left out something that could be vital. What his mother said reminded him. In spite of his swift response to the emergency, someone else had beaten him to it. Someone who must have spotted the fire before Duncan and Mace did. Spotted, or set it?

Roz, on her way upstairs, must have seen something in his expression, because she stopped on the step below him. They were eye to eye.

"What?" she asked.

"Somebody knew about the fire before I did. Someone had already called it in."

"Tracy. Or her uncle?"

Duncan shook his head. "Tracy didn't know about it yet. Astrid called across the road to the Mattos farm because she heard something, or someone, out back. So Tracy called me, and I told her to send her uncle. We got there sort of at the same time. I told him to call 911, but he went to the barn, not the house. I saw him there later."

"So ... someone else saw the fire way back there ..." Roz spoke slowly, feeling her way. "Unless they knew about it because they set it."

"Why would they set it and then call the fire department?" Duncan asked her.

"Maybe they just wanted to scare Mrs. Valentine," Roz suggested.

"But why?" Duncan said. "It's so dangerous. Look what it did to her."

"Maybe they wanted her out of there," said Roz. "And, look, she is."

Frowning, Duncan sank down on the top step to think this through. "It was a man," he said. "I'm pretty sure they said it was a man."

Roz sat, too, her back to the banister. "Do you suppose Curt Barrington or that Officer Keezer even thought about this?" she asked.

Duncan shrugged.

"Want to try it on Dad?" Roz suggested.

"Me? No," Duncan retorted.

"But you're the one that was told about the previous caller," Roz pointed out.

Duncan shook his head. "I can't. Dad's too … All he has to do is look at me and he goes ballistic."

"Okay!" Roz declared, pulling herself up. "I guess it's up to me." Making a face that actually made Duncan smile, she went back downstairs and into the kitchen.

Duncan waited where he was. He didn't try to discern individual words or phrases that came to him from the kitchen. Instead he listened to the rising pitch, the abrupt interruptions, the descent in volume, the next upsurge. Then everything grew quieter and he heard his father in his louder telephone voice say, "Curt? One thought here. Yes. Sorry, yes, it's Rick Veerick. Do you keep a record of calls that come in? Well, like the call that reported the fire before Duncan called in on Astrid's phone. Yes. Well, Natalie and I were just wondering if you'd identified that caller. The phone service said it was a man. Yes. Right. Just, you know, just curious. Thanks, Curt. Good night."

Duncan sat awhile pondering who the unknown caller could have been. When Roz came back upstairs he was still sitting there. "Thanks," he said to her.

"You owe me big-time," she told him with a grin. "Now everyone's got something else to chew over."

"Thanks," he said again. "Really."

"You'll be all right," she assured him as she stepped over his legs. "They'll give you a hard time until they get tired of running their crime investigation without a suspect. Then they'll leave you alone."

How could she be so sure? he wondered. All she knew of this sort of thing was from the tube or the movies.

Back in his room, Duncan surveyed the chaos left by the searchers. They had invaded and transformed his private world, so that he was a stranger here, someone other people had constructed out of random bits and pieces called evidence.

Was all of this real or virtual? Either way, it would be a good time for some detective hero to show up and break the case wide open.

During the first part of the week, Duncan was called out of class three times. Lois Firth, who turned out to be a social worker from the state juvenile crime unit, also spoke with other kids and some of Duncan's teachers. She kept looking for different ways to get him to open up about his relationship with Astrid and how he'd gained her trust. Of course he must have felt imposed on. Had he been resentful enough to want to, well, get back at Mrs. Valentine? You know, scare her or maybe even destroy some of her belongings?

When Duncan shook his head, Lois Firth said it would help him to talk about how he felt. At that point he nearly told her that being singled out like this in school sucked, but he just said he felt okay.

It was obvious that no detective was coming forward to nail the firebug. That left Duncan where he'd been since Sunday, along with "proof" that he'd been ripping off Astrid and plenty of hearsay evidence that he'd wormed his way into her affections. Duncan informed his parents that he shouldn't be made to go to school. "Half the kids won't talk to me, and the other half stare at me like I'm some kind of freak." Of course he exaggerated. Neil set an example, and a few kids went out of their way to be decent. But Duncan couldn't avoid the fallout from all the law-enforcement activity.

By now he was barely sleeping at night. After the rest of the family went to bed, he would leave his trashed room and sack out on the couch.

Thursday night, when another thunderstorm swept through Chiswick, he woke up in the living room wondering whether he'd remembered to warn Tom Lassiter and Emmy that Mo might take off. Lying awake, Duncan recalled Astrid's brassy answer to thunder. Did turning up the volume on a trumpet fanfare really work for a dog? Or was that music as much a comfort to Astrid as a way to block the terror for Mo?

The more he thought about it, the more he was convinced that he'd forgotten to mention Mo's phobia. If only he could call Tom and Emmy right now before anything bad happened. But it was the middle of the night, and he was in enough trouble already.

As the storm subsided, he drifted into sleep. So it wasn't until he was packing up his homework for school the next morning that he remembered the math test. Well, he thought drearily, he might not flunk, but he wouldn't ace it either.

The test was a drag, but at least he got through the day without being hauled into the principal's office for more questioning. This Friday they'd get out of school early, too. He still might make it through to the end of the year. And while it was still on his mind, he'd call as soon as he got home and leave a message about Mo's thunder phobia.

Tracy wouldn't leave him alone, though. As they headed up Garnet Road, she started yammering about his predicament.

"They probably won't arrest you," she declared. "On account of that phone call. Dad says they have the recorded voice. And the time. So you're almost off the hook."

"Almost?" he said.

"Well, you're still the number-one suspect," she told him. "They can't agree on the motive. One state police officer thinks you started the fire so you could be a hero and rescue Astrid. What a creep!"

Since that sounded like Lois Firth, Duncan said, "She's not bad. She's just into relationships. Like friendship isn't what you think; it's dependency. And trust is control."

Tracy said, "They probably can't decide whether Astrid told you to burn the mummy and then the fire got out of hand, or whether you've been stealing from her for someone else to sell stuff."

Duncan nodded. When he heard it put like that, either take seemed reasonable. He said, "Someone torched the chicken house, and we still don't know why."

"So let's find out," Tracy suggested.

He refrained from telling her that they weren't in a television crime show. She was on his side, and she knew a lot more than he did about the rest of Chiswick. He said, "What makes you think we can?"

They were passing her driveway, but she kept on walking along with him. A tractor droned in a field nearby, and they could hear it gear down as it climbed uphill. Tracy said, "We should look back over everything we've seen and heard all along."

He said, "The state police and fire marshals have gone all over the shed and house as well as the fire site."

"But we were there first," she reminded him.

Whatever that meant, thought Duncan. He was fed up. He didn't want to think about it anymore.

Just then Mo came dashing onto the road from Astrid's house and hurtling toward them.

"Mo!" Duncan called. He picked the little dog up and submitted to the frantic wet-tongue greeting. As they came abreast of the house, he could see that the front door was open.

Eddie emerged with a suitcase and set it down on the granite step. "Foolish dog doesn't know when it's well off," he said to Duncan. "Can you get him back to the new place? I need to hit the road."

He disappeared inside the house. A moment later he came out with his laptop and a cardboard box, which he carried down to the car parked at the end of the driveway.

Duncan held on to the wriggling dog and said, "Mo's not foolish, just scared of thunder."

"Whatever," Eddie replied as he returned for the suitcase on the step. "I'd appreciate it if you'd take him off my hands." He made one more trip inside for boxes, set them down while he locked the front door, and finished packing his car. "By the way, Duncan," he called as he started the car, "any idea where Astrid keeps her cash?"

Duncan told him about the wad of bills in the vegetable drawer of the refrigerator.

"Oh," said Eddie. "I was sure I'd left her plenty of money, but then I couldn't find it."

The car backed out of the driveway and headed down Garnet Road.

"Stupid!" Tracy said. "What did you tell him that for? He's setting you up."

"No, he's not. What do you mean?"

"You want to bet he'll be on the phone with Mr. Barrington? You wait. They'll be on your case about the missing money."

"So what?" Duncan responded. "It's hopeless anyway. They never believe kids. Never."

Tracy began to smile. "Maybe we can beat the nephew at his own game. Come with me, Duncan. We need to get my folks on this. Come on."

"What about Mo?" he asked. "I should call Tom Lassiter and Emmy."

"So call them from my house. Come on. We're going to turn things around."

"What if the nephew was on the level?" Duncan asked.

"Then he'll understand. Listen, Duncan, we've got to move quickly."

Duncan went with her because he couldn't resist the force of her confidence. Even if she was way wrong, she was fighting for him. He wasn't so stupid as to ignore that.

Mace Mattos was coming out of the farmhouse as they were going in. "What's up?" he asked. He looked to Duncan as though the last thing he wanted was to hear their reply.

But Tracy answered quickly, "Somthing weird across the road."

Mace Mattos stopped. "Weird how?" he asked.

Tracy said, "The nephew tried to get Duncan in trouble. I need Mom and Dad."

"Wanda went into Brixton. Bud's out in the cornfield. What's the nephew up to?"

Before Tracy could finish telling him, her uncle had reversed his direction and was leading them into the house. Tracy tried to explain what ought to be done, but Mace Mattos gestured for quiet. Listening to him on the phone, they could tell he was speaking to a machine.

"It's Mace Mattos, Curt. We're kind of curious about whether Astrid's nephew contacted you in the last few minutes. He just asked Duncan Veerick about some missing money."

Tracy tried to correct her uncle. "Asked where Astrid kept it," she whispered.

Mace tried to brush Tracy off. "Seems like he was setting a trap," he said into the phone. "Could be wrong about that. But if he's spoken to you or left a message just ahead of my call, or if he reaches you in the next few minutes, you might want to look into it." He hung up. "Tracy, will you butt out when I'm trying to raise a red flag? If Curt follows up on this, you can tell him your whole story."

Duncan was going over in his mind what Astrid had said to him, and now he nodded and nodded.

"What?" Tracy demanded.

Duncan said, "You're right. It's coming back. Astrid was on the bed and you were in the living room. Astrid didn't want you to see where the money came from. 'Eddie's hiding place,' she said. 'Eddie's home bank.' So just now Eddie wanted me to admit that I knew. With you to witness." Duncan looked at Tracy. "But why now?"

"Why pin the fire on me first time around?" Mace Mattos said. "Not because he had anything against me. Because I was conveniently there. It helped that I was plastered and couldn't remember much."

"But Duncan and I could," Tracy said. "I told Mr. Barrington it couldn't be you. So did Duncan. So why did the nephew take aim at you and then at Duncan?"

Mace Mattos sat down at the dining room table and scowled at a plate with a last slice of banana bread and a lot of crumbs. Slowly he shook his head. "I don't like this," he said. "I don't like stirring all this up. Wait and see if the nephew made that call." Absently he picked up the slice and stuffed it into his mouth. Then he got up and walked out of the house.

Tracy and Duncan sat in silence. Mo strained toward the nearly empty plate, but Duncan held him tight.

Then Tracy said, "We can't let things just happen anymore and not do anything." She got up and went into the kitchen. He heard her open and slam a cabinet door. Something rustled. He looked around the living room. Maybe he should go home. He stared at a lamp made from an old-fashioned butter churn and then at the mantelpiece adorned with framed photographs and the statue of a Holstein cow.

Tracy returned with a pad and a bottle of Coke under one arm, a bag of corn chips and two glasses in her hands.

"You take the pad. There's a pencil on the table. Sit there." She poured out Coke, shoved the chips toward him, and said, "So get going. Write down the name of everyone you know involved with Mrs. Valentine." She looked over at the pad. "Not like that, Duncan. Make a chart."

"What for?" he asked. She hadn't said anything about a chart.

"To eliminate suspects."

"Like Doris?"

"Well, maybe not Doris. Try men. To be systematic. The nephew's the obvious suspect, so begin with him. You need two columns." Tracy sounded absolutely sure of herself. "One for positive things about each of them and the other for negatives."

Duncan scowled. "What other suspects are there? I don't know any."

"You sure? What about the guy that did the appraisal?"

"Okay, him. But he was barely … Well, he took the stoves. That's all."

"Fine. Put him down."

"Stan. Stan something. I don't know anything about him. Stan Brecher."

"See?" she told him. "Now you're beginning to remember more."

Duncan wrote, "Knew Valentines from way back. Friendly."

"That's it?"

"Well, he came when he heard about the fire. Gave me a ride."

"Negatives?" Tracy prompted.

"I think he wanted to buy the mummy. He asked Eddie, who didn't know anything about it. So why would he burn it?"

"What else?"

"Well, he had some deal going with Eddie. It might have had to do with the appraisal or the stoves." Duncan was trying to recall the scrap of conversation he'd overheard between Eddie and Stan. "Eddie was annoyed with him. Maybe just because he was upset about Astrid."

"Let's go on to him, then. To the nephew."

Duncan ate a corn chip and let Mo lick his fingers. In the positive column he wrote, "Didn't blame me about the mummy." He felt foolish doing this. Then he wrote, "Put money in Astrid's account so she could pay bills."

Tracy pulled her chair around to sit beside him. "What about negative things?"

"I'm doing the positives first," he said. He thought a moment before writing, "Tried to warn Astrid about theft."

"Is that positive?" Tracy asked him.

Duncan nodded. "To protect her, alert her to danger." He thought a moment. "Oh, you mean it scared her. But maybe she needed to be scared."

Tracy just looked at him.

"All right, then. I'll put it in the negative side, too." After writing, he said, "I think we should be looking at motives."

"That's what we're doing," Tracy told him.

Duncan shook his head. "Not like this. We've got to figure out what was in it for him." He threw down the pencil. "It's pointless, though. He was hundreds of miles away."

Tracy said, "You'd make a lousy detective."

He shrugged.

She said, "I bet it took him less than a minute to find someone to do it for him. For a price. We'll work on that next."

By now Duncan was following his own line of thinking. "Maybe Eddie Shoop arranged for a fire to scare his aunt into moving."

Tracy nodded. "Then he'd get his hands on everything. But why? He was already running the show, wasn't he?"

Duncan frowned. "Eddie wanted Astrid safe. I don't think he faked the way he felt. What if we're on the wrong track?"

"Don't you back down now," Tracy retorted. "You stick with this and find out what he was up to."

"If anything," he responded.

"You know what a victimless crime is?" she asked him.

"Sort of," he said. "Like cheating or not paying taxes?"

"What if the fire was supposed to be that kind?"

"But Astrid was a victim!" Duncan exclaimed.

Tracy nodded. "Maybe not on purpose. Afterward it changed what the crime was. Afterward. Then what was the victimless crime for? Was getting everything insured part of it? And those overpriced bids. Maybe they could be used when he reported his loss. We should find out what they were all about. If you still have a key, we could look for the stuff I saw."

He shook his head. It would be just his luck to be caught snooping in Astrid's house.

Another approach sprang to mind. "The website! It should have prices, even links that might show us what Eddie was really up to."

Tracy grinned. "Not bad. You're catching on," she said. "Let's go for it."

Tracy took Duncan upstairs to what she called the sewing room. The computer was next to the sewing machine. She began to search for Eddie's website.

After a while Duncan set Mo down and tried a different approach. He started with salvage, then narrowed the subject to New England and antiques. He found a few businesses with pictures displaying fixtures like those in the shed across the road. Perhaps Eddie used them as models for his site. But where was it?

Duncan started over, beginning with the name: Valentine. Sure enough, a few promising links cropped up from other sites. But they all led to dead ends.

He pushed back his chair and shook his head. The website Eddie had created as a marketing vehicle seemed to have vanished.

"Don't give up," Tracy told Duncan. "Remember, there's printouts, a paper trail."

He got up and headed for the stairs. He said, "Doris cleaned up after Astrid was taken to the hospital. Eddie blasted her for trashing his papers."

"Sounds like they were important to him."

"Well, he'd brought them with him. He didn't have a printer here." Duncan added, "You know, we might be way off base."

"What do you mean?" she asked, following him. "Why?"

Mo scrambled after them, skidding down the stairs. Duncan blocked his descent and picked him up. "We haven't heard from Curt Barrington. That could mean that Eddie didn't call in about the hidden money, that he wasn't trying to trap me."

"It could also mean that Mr. Barrington hasn't gotten his messages yet. You're not quitting, are you?"

Duncan shrugged, unsure. But once he and the little dog were out on the road, he found himself making his own balance sheet on Eddie. There were too many contradictory pieces to this puzzle. Why would Eddie go out of his way to implicate him when he was already under suspicion?

At home Mo headed for the kitchen. Duncan followed. Suddenly he felt ravenous. He'd left this morning without breakfast and skipped lunch. He couldn't be sure about last night's supper either. Now he ached for food.

Opening the refrigerator, he scanned the ordinary items inside—butter, muffins, eggs, salad stuff, carrots, juice, yogurt, milk. What a contrast with the contents of Astrid's fridge with its rotting greens, its packet of money. He fried up three eggs, made toast, and heated water for instant cocoa.

Mo watched, rapt, his eyes following every gesture. Duncan shared a crust with Mo and let him have the last bite of egg. After that, he took the rest of his cocoa into the living room and stretched out on his father's recliner. Mo jumped up and nestled beside him.

Roz came home to find them snoozing there. When she made a fuss over the little dog, Mo abandoned his cushy perch and went straight to her. Right before Duncan's eyes Mo was becoming the well-mannered house pet he had found at the Lassiter house.

Only then did he realize that Mo had reverted to his older ways as soon as he'd run to Duncan on the road. Maybe it shouldn't be all that surprising that Astrid's familiar could switch personalities like that.

"Messages here," said Roz, going to the phone. "Did you call those dog people?"

"Who? Oh. No, not yet." Groaning, he sat up.

"From Emmy," Roz told him, writing down a number. "Twice. Want to call her now before I get going?" Roz was already putting in the call, but she handed the phone to him.

A machine invited him to leave a message, so he told it that he'd found Mo at Astrid's house and the dog was now home with him. They could come for him anytime this evening.

Before Roz shut herself away with the phone, she asked Duncan whether he'd thought about keeping Mo himself.

He shook his head. Then he said, "Those people are great for him."

Roz said, "They let him run away."

"My fault," Duncan told her. "I never warned them about thunderstorms."

Roz turned on him. "Stop it! Why do you always put yourself down? You need to stick up for yourself."

"I'm about to do just that," he told her, a bit surprised at how determined he sounded. Well, why not? He wasn't quitting. That much was clear to him now.

"Good," she said. "You don't deserve all this crap they've been dumping on you."

"I know," he agreed. "Still, I've been stupid. I know that, too."

The phone was already in Roz's clutches when it rang. He said, "That might be Tom Lassiter for me."

Handing him the phone, she told him to be quick about it.

"Like you?" he asked with a taunting grin.

She made a face at him, which he barely noticed. He was listening to a weeping Doris Beasley inform him that Astrid Valentine had just died.

"She wasn't alone," Doris told Duncan. "I was with her. I held her hand."

Duncan walked Mo down to the Valentine house.
He wasn't sure whether he needed to do this for the dog or for himself. Maybe he'd put him over the fence and give him one last playtime in his yard.

But he didn't get that far because a truck was backed up to the shed. He wasn't quite sure what he ought to do. Call out? Just quietly leave? While he stood there undecided, a man came through the shed door lugging a heavy sack.

"Eddie Shoop isn't here," Duncan called.

The man said, "I know that. I'm clearing out some hardware for him." Then he looked up, and Duncan saw that it was Stan Brecher. "Oh, hello again," Stan Brecher said. "Astrid's young friend."

Mo, responding to the cordial tone, trotted over to the truck.

Stan Brecher leaned against the tailgate with the bag propped beside him. "So you found her dog after all. That must please her."

"She doesn't know. Didn't know," Duncan said, suddenly finding it hard to speak. "She's dead," he blurted. "Just. Today."

Stan Brecher shoved the sack back on the truck bed and came toward Duncan. "I had no idea," he said. "I mean, Eddie told me she was in a bad way, but ..." He paused. "I've known her a long time."

Duncan drew a deep breath and said, "I wanted someone to bring Mo to her. I promised I'd find him. Mo. The dog."

Stan Brecher nodded. "Tough," he said. "Tough having her count on you like that."

Duncan could only nod.

Stan Brecher said, "You shouldn't pay any mind to what people are saying about the fire. You were a good friend to her." He stood a moment longer. Then when Duncan said nothing, he turned away and went back to removing antique hardware from the shed.

Duncan watched in disbelief. He seemed to be floating, suspended between two opposing views of Stan Brecher. Tracy's positive and negative columns were useless; they left too much out. Could this kindly man have cut a deal to torch the chicken house? Here he was, calmly removing hardware from the fire-damaged shed, at ease with the task. Then what about that exchange that Duncan had nearly walked in on, Stan Brecher weakly defending himself to Eddie? A deal gone bad? That was what Duncan had thought then. Now he had to wonder: what deal? Suppose Stan had agreed to torch the chicken house. Would he go through with it even if it meant burning up the mummy?

Watching him haul another sack, Duncan had to fight off the urge to come right out and ask him what had ticked off Eddie. Assuming that the fire had been Eddie's brainchild. Had Eddie ordered up a harmless fire, quickly reported? For what purpose? An insurance scam? Or to unsettle Astrid even more than she already was? But Eddie was genuinely attached to Astrid. Wasn't he?

Then what about Stan Brecher? Could Duncan find out anything without sending him scrambling to cover his tracks? Duncan couldn't just ask him how he'd heard about the fire in time to show up that same night. Maybe just get him talking about it?

Duncan walked over to the truck and waited beside the tailgate. When Stan returned with another sack of hardware, Duncan spoke up. "Did you know about the mummy?"

Stan heaved the sack onto the truck bed. "Astrid said the mummies were long gone. I figured Paul might've stashed away one or two somewhere." He shrugged. "I let it go. Then an old customer surfaced. I asked Eddie, who didn't know anything about them. Come to find out there was one in the fire." Stan shook his head. "Big loss. Big waste."

"Do you think someone wanted it burned?" Duncan asked.

"Oh, no," Stan replied. "It was worth a bundle. They'd never guess it was there."

"Wouldn't they see it?" Duncan asked.

Stan shook his head. "In a storm? Wasn't it dark?"

"I guess," Duncan answered.

"Know what I think?" Stan said. "I think they didn't have a clue. Probably they thought setting that fire was no big deal. Probably."

Duncan nodded. "That's what I think too," he said, turning away and calling to Mo, who was scratching at the fence to get into his yard.

Duncan walked up the road. Mo kept running ahead and doubling back as though hurrying him along.

After speaking with Stan, Duncan was pretty sure he was closing in on the answers he needed. Unless he was too late. Inside his house, he went straight to the telephone. Would Doris be home yet? Getting a busy signal, he kept trying until finally he got through. He had to check the rush of words that nearly burst out of him. Keep a lid on it, he told himself.

"I'm sorry to bother you at a time like this," he said. The sound of his own voice grated in his ears.

"What is it?" Doris asked. "Is it about Astrid?" She blew her nose.

"Yes," he said tightly. "Sort of. There were papers in her living room. I was wondering." He stopped to catch his breath. "Do you know what happened to them?"

For a moment he thought the line had gone dead. Then Doris said, "I brought trash bags, the heavy-duty black kind. They were already in my car when the nephew showed up." She paused. "Let me think. I drop off the garbage at the landfill most Saturdays."

Duncan was pressing the phone so hard against his head that his ear throbbed.

"I'm not sure. I think the bags with plastic for recycling and paper are still out back. Yes, from when I cleared out Astrid's living room. Why?"

Duncan exhaled. He could feel his fingers relax, his jaw slacken, his teeth unclench. "I'd like to go through the bag of paper. Could I come? I think I can get someone to drive me over."

"No need, Duncan," she told him. "I'm coming to Astrid's first thing tomorrow. I'm going to pick up something nice for her to wear. I told the funeral director I'd take care of it. The nephew doesn't know that she used to care about her looks. I don't imagine it matters to him. Anyway, I'll drop off the bag. I hope you find what you're looking for."

"Thank you," he said. "I hope so too."

After he put down the phone, he rubbed his ear and then his fingers. He had never felt like this before. When he climbed, he was always acutely aware of the strain of grip and balance. At least clinging to rock was hard and definite. Seeking and holding on to uncertain motives and shifting clues was more like clutching air.

Waiting was awful. Duncan kept telling himself that if it turned out he was way off base about the deal between Eddie and Stan, the printouts he was aching to examine would amount to nothing. Still, there had to be some reason for Eddie to have jacked up the prices on everything. What if his scheme was all about helping Astrid, seeing to it that she cashed in on the contents of the shed and house? Did his motive make a difference? Duncan supposed so. Then he reminded himself that as long as he was on the hot seat, he couldn't afford to let questions like this distract him.

Later that evening, when Tom Lassiter and Emmy came for Mo, Duncan felt oddly distanced from the reunion. Not that he failed to notice Mo's ecstatic greeting or that afterward the little dog scooted off to bestow affection on everyone else.

"Are you sure it's all right if we take him?" Tom asked. He looked at Duncan, who nodded.

Mo on a leash lunged through the open door without a backward glance.

As soon as the door was shut, Roz turned on her parents. "Whatever happened to sticking up for your own kid?" she demanded.

"What?" Dad exclaimed. "What do you mean?"

"Didn't it occur to you or Mom that Duncan's been taking care of that dog for months and might have feelings?"

"It's all right," Duncan said. "Really."

"Duncan has a lot on his plate right now," Mom told Roz. "He doesn't need ... complications."

"Complications?" Roz exclaimed. "Is that what you call letting half the town run over him?"

Dad flushed. "Aren't you overdoing the drama, Roz?" he asked, making an effort to sound calm. "If Duncan had been more forthcoming, he might've spared himself some embarrassment. Which, by the way, affects more than him. Don't forget I have a business to run."

"It's worse than embarrassment," Roz retorted. "He'll start high school with ... with—"

"It's all right," Duncan repeated before Roz made things worse. If she accused them of failing to trust their own son, he might be dragged into it, and he wasn't ready for that.

His mother reached out to Roz. "It's wonderful to hear you stick up for your brother," she said. "I'm proud of you."

Roz stepped back, glaring.

"The important thing is that there may not be any formal charges," Mom said. "We've been assured—"

"Say his name!" Roz shouted. "Say 'Duncan.' Say 'They can't prove that Duncan is an arsonist,' or whatever they call it."

Dad said, "Enough, Roz. This has been hard on every one of us. We ought to think of Astrid, who has passed on. We should respect her memory."

On that heavy note Duncan and Roz withdrew to the front hall.

"Want to come along with Denny and me tonight?" Roz asked. "A bunch of us are going to the movies."

Duncan was tempted. But he shook his head. "Thanks. I'm

fine. I'm just going to chill, maybe do some catch-up on math. I forgot I had a test today. I screwed up."

"So you're human," Roz said. "No big deal."

He went up to his room, which was still in shambles from the police. They had ransacked his closet and every drawer, probably looking for more stuff from the Valentine house. Maybe they expected to find a trace of gasoline on a sleeve.

It occurred to him that his mother used to get after him to clean up messes that were nothing compared with this. And no quick fixes, she'd insist, like pulling the bedspread over tangled sheets and discarded clothes. One glance at the bed and she would remind him that before it could be set to rights it must be unmade.

Had she left this mess alone because of what it signified? Or was that his take? It seemed to him that if the upheaval in his room stood for anything, it had to be for his own unmaking.

He couldn't tell whether he'd end up keeping most of these scattered belongings. Probably he wouldn't know until he was ready to dig in and deal with the chaos.

Not yet, he thought. Not quite yet.

All the same he dropped down on his hands and knees to look for his method book under clothes emptied out of drawers, behind books and video games dumped from shelves, amid nuts and cams and other climbing devices, all of these overspread with found objects from roadsides and trails and plowed fields that he'd been collecting all his life.

Early Saturday morning Doris Beasley dropped off the bag of paper trash. "It's everything that was scattered all over the place," she told Duncan before he carried it into the wood-shed. "I was trying to set things to rights, but the nephew was furious. I offered to help him sort through it before I dumped it at the landfill, but he just stormed off."

Duncan's mother, who had come downstairs behind him, saw who was at the door and said, "Oh, Doris, I'm so sorry. Please come in. How about a cup of coffee?"

Duncan had managed to get the bag out of sight, but he couldn't be sure Doris wouldn't mention why she'd dropped by. He could only hope they'd just talk about Astrid. He didn't want anyone else pawing through the papers until he'd had a good look.

So he started right in, upending the bag and spreading its contents all around him. Junk and more junk, he thought as he kicked the papers this way and that. There was a familiar-looking invoice with coffee stains. Many invoices. He crouched down to read dates. Price quotes, yes. He couldn't tell what might be sig-nificant. He'd save everything just in case.

Then, as he flattened one folded sheet of paper after another, he came upon a few that were folded in half rather than in thirds for mailing. He spread one of them out. It was a printout of an e-mail that included previous correspondence with names and addresses. So far so good. Now he had some of Eddie's contacts.

He pounced on other print-sized papers that were folded that way. Folded for keeping, he guessed, not for mailing. Here was something called "Claim Draft #2." It appeared to contain segments of the inventory. An itemized list of plumbing fixtures looked familiar. So far everything here seemed on the level. Looking for more papers related to the claim, Duncan turned up a copy of an insurance form. More lists, all thoroughly documented with appraised value. Everything appeared to be in order.

Duncan sat back on his heels. Any of these papers could shed light on something later on, revealing a slip or discrepancy. If only he knew what to look for.

He was just stacking the printouts when he came across a cover letter for the insurance form. It seemed to be perfectly business-like. No, not quite. It lacked a date. Was there a date on the form? He shuffled back to it. The small box for the date was blank. Not that it meant anything. But he might as well check out "Claim Draft #2." No date here either. He supposed it would take days for Eddie Shoop to identify all the items to be listed. He would date the claim when he was ready to send it off.

Duncan was still peering at Claim Draft #2 when it suddenly came to him that e-mails were always dated. The cover letter and the form were dateless, but Claim Draft #2 was different. Eddie Shoop had sent it to himself. Before the fire. The mailing date showed that. Duncan couldn't be sure, but he guessed that this claim draft pre-dated Stan's so-called appraisal as well.

Stunned, Duncan could feel the blood rush to his head. It was almost as though he had caught himself in Eddie's deceit. At first he didn't know what to do. He tried to sort the papers, but he kept dropping them. So he just sat there with them until he heard

Doris drive away. Then he shoved everything except the claim draft and cover letter and insurance form back in the bag and wedged it behind a stack of kindling.

He ran all the way down to the farm. The Mattos dog, objecting to his sudden appearance, barked and advanced toward him with upraised tail and hackles. Duncan tried to calm the dog. Tracy's father stepped out of the barn, saw Duncan, and told the dog to go lie down.

"Everything all right?" Bud Mattos asked as Tracy appeared behind him.

"Yes," Duncan said. "I think so."

Tracy told her father she'd just be a minute, and he went back inside.

"So?" she demanded as soon as they were alone.

He held out the papers. He knew he was grinning like an idiot.

She beamed. "Doris delivered the goods!"

He nodded. Let Tracy play hot-shot detective all she liked.

She said, "An insurance scam?"

"I think so. Maybe more than that. There's too much … Eddie was working on a claim before the fire, like he knew it was going to happen. And he kept price quotes and orders from his website. I can't be sure, but I think he was selling stuff he was writing claims on."

"Listen, Duncan," she said. "I have to go back to work with Dad."

He had to think fast. "What about these papers?" he asked her. "Can you keep them for now? We should get copies for backup, but I don't know where."

Tracy nodded. "You're right," she said. "They'll be safe in my room. Is this all?"

"No, there's tons more. We can look through everything after the weekend. My parents don't know I have the stuff."

Clutching the papers, Tracy took off, pounding heavily up to her house.

Duncan headed for the road. He could hear Tracy's father calling from the barn. He hurried on.

As soon as he walked through the front door he smelled bacon. Suddenly he was ravenous. He found his father in the kitchen making pancakes.

"Just in time," Dad said. "Where were you off to?"

"I had to take something to the farm," Duncan answered, picking up a slice of bacon.

His mother said, "You missed Doris. Oh, no, you were leaving just as she came. Well, you missed her visit. She needed to talk about Astrid."

Duncan nodded. It sounded as though the paper delivery had gone unmentioned.

They were just sitting down to breakfast when a car drove up. Mom glanced out the window. "Oh, no," she said. "Curt. What now?"

Dad got up. "I'll go," he said. A moment later Duncan heard him saying, "You sure I can't offer you some breakfast?"

Curt followed Dad into the kitchen. "Sorry to interrupt," he said. "I just have a few questions for Duncan."

Duncan saw the look of alarm that passed between his parents. This time he didn't feel it himself. He poured more maple syrup on his pancakes and watched it soak in.

Maybe just to keep busy, his mother went to the cupboard for another coffee mug, which she filled and set down in front of Curt Barrington.

"Did you have a conversation with Eddie Shoop yesterday?" Curt asked Duncan.

Duncan swallowed a mouthful of pancake and nodded.

"Can you tell me what was said?"

"He wanted me to take care of the dog." Duncan was in no hurry to continue. He was startled by the anger that swept through him. "Eddie also asked if I knew where Astrid kept her money. I told him. Afterward I remembered that Astrid said it was Eddie's hiding place. Eddie's bank. That's what she called it."

Curt Barrington sipped his coffee before asking Duncan if he'd taken money from it.

Prepared for that question, Duncan replied almost cheerfully, "I did."

"How many times?" the constable asked.

"Once," Duncan said. He realized that his parents' breakfasts were untouched. "If you don't want your pancakes … ," he said to his father, shoving his empty plate toward him.

"How much?" came the next predictable question.

"I've no idea," Duncan said. "I gave it to Astrid so she could pay Tracy and me. She took out some bills. Then I put the rest back."

Curt Barrington sighed. "Why do you think Eddie Shoop asked you about missing money, about where Astrid kept it?"

Duncan pushed back from the table and carried his plate to the stove. He looked in the oven. "Are we saving these for Roz?" he asked his father, indicating extra pancakes keeping warm.

"Go ahead," Dad said. "I can make more if she wants them. If she ever gets up."

Duncan helped himself and brought his plate to the table. He looked at Curt Barrington. Grief for Astrid and outrage at Eddie and resentment at most of the adults in his life all came boiling up at once. "What difference does it make what I think?" he asked.

"Duncan!" his father exclaimed. "If you can't be helpful, at least don't be rude."

Duncan caught himself just in time. He knew how dangerously close he'd come to losing it. He couldn't bellow like Astrid. He mustn't strike out. All he needed to do was wait for the truth to come out. So he drew a long breath and said, "I'm sorry. I guess I'm tired of not being believed."

Curt Barrington nodded. "That's understandable," he said. "But you've got to see how things appear to us." He stood up. He said, "Thanks, Natalie, Rick. Thanks, Duncan. Why don't we pick up on this later on?" It wasn't really a question, but a statement of intent.

Fine, thought Duncan. As soon as he had copies of Eddie's printouts, he'd hand the originals over to Curt Barrington. Then he could answer his own questions.

After Duncan's father had walked the constable to the door, he returned to the kitchen and sat down to his cold pancakes.

Duncan's mother said quietly, "You've changed, Duncan. I hadn't realized how much." She sounded sad. "I wish I understood where we went wrong."

Duncan's father reached across the table and took her hand. "Maybe Duncan will tell us what he didn't want to say to Curt."

That was smart, thought Duncan, surprised that his father got that much. He said, "It's not all your fault. You went along with what you thought was evidence. What everyone else decided."

"I believed in your truthfulness until things just mounted up," said his mother.

"Things," Duncan said. "Here's basic math: Zero plus zero equals zero."

"Not all zeroes," his father pointed out. "What about the bone thing they found in your room?"

"It was mine," Duncan said. "Astrid picked it out for me. The owl. She said it would grow on me. I was going to hang it on my wall."

"Oh, Duncan! Why didn't you tell us?" his mother asked.

"When not one person ever believed that Astrid wanted me to bring all the other carved bones here for safekeeping?"

They sat in silence, not eating. They heard Roz coming downstairs.

She poked her head into the kitchen and said, "What's this? A funeral? Oh, sorry, Duncan. Really, I am. Like you need anyone else in this family not thinking."

He guessed he was ready now. While they were all together. The time had come to share his news.

Curt Barrington and the others were so confident of the information they gleaned from Eddie Shoop's printouts that they could afford to defer immediate action. Meanwhile, the evidence would be turned over to the insurance company because of financial considerations.

"Financial considerations?" Tracy railed. "What about justice?"

Duncan thought what she really meant was revenge. By now his rage had cooled. He didn't especially relish what was to come. No one doubted that Eddie Shoop would try to save himself by exposing the person who had set the chicken house on fire. Eddie had no idea, and wouldn't find out until much later, that he was up against overwhelming proof of his scam to sell fixtures and art objects he claimed as losses.

None of this was generally known yet. Out of respect for Astrid, local authorities attempted to keep things quiet until after her funeral. The two families on Garnet Road were asked to keep to themselves what they already knew, even though this meant that almost everyone in school still assumed that Duncan was a suspect.

He tried not to let it get to him, but he couldn't help feeling burned, as if he'd actually been seared by the hen house fire. While he played in every extra band rehearsal, he refused to consider attending the eighth-grade graduation party.

First Roz and then Neil tried to talk him into going, but he held firm. Roz, the image maker, insisted that other kids' opinions didn't matter, especially since he was about to be cleared. He managed not to laugh.

A week before graduation Eddie Shoop returned to Chiswick to bury his aunt.

Duncan had practiced "When the Saints Go Marching In" so that he'd be prepared in case Eddie happened to know that Astrid had wanted it.

Duncan actually mentioned it to Eddie early on the morning of the funeral, a day full of birdsong and the heady scent of cut grass and spring flowers.

"I don't think so, Duncan," Eddie Shoop responded, sounding cool. "Under the circumstances."

Not many people attended the graveside service, but the neighbors were there as well as Doris Beasley and a few old friends and associates from Astrid's past. Duncan caught sight of Stan Brecher, who looked ill at ease in his shirt and tie and clean church trousers.

Doris whispered to Mom and Wanda Mattos that she had wanted Eddie to invite the guests to Astrid's house for sandwiches and coffee, which she'd offered to prepare. But he had turned her down.

"Never mind," Wanda whispered in return. "We'll go to our house. We can throw together a light lunch. It's the people that matter, not the place."

Eddie showed up briefly at the Mattos farm, then left to deal with a pile of last-minute tasks before taking off for Brixton to talk to the real estate agent. A few of the older friends stopped by, though not Stan Brecher. People told each other stories about the

Valentines and ate the pickup lunch and then began to leave.

Doris Beasley, who helped clean up in the kitchen, was one of the last to go.

As soon as she was out of the house, Wanda Mattos said, "I wish we could've told her what's going on with the nephew."

Duncan's mother said, "It's bound to come out soon."

Duncan started to speak, then thought better of it. He was pretty sure Doris already knew, though whether from her own shrewd guesswork or because someone had already decided to bring her into the loop, he couldn't tell.

Tracy said, "I know what you're thinking."

Duncan laughed. "Want to bet?"

Tracy shook her head. "Anyway," she told him, "I'd say you're right."

He wasn't even tempted to ask her what she thought he was right about. One thing he'd learned from their collaboration was that her clueless image was deceptive. It might even be deliberate. He wouldn't put anything past her.

Commencement Day at Chiswick Middle School

was a major happening in town.

The band performed before the ceremony. Duncan played his best, trying to keep the trumpet from overwhelming other instruments. Holding back like that also helped to make wrong notes less obvious.

Afterward his parents mingled and chatted awhile. Duncan packed up his trumpet, handed his diploma over to his mother, and then hung around until they were ready to leave. Since they still had half a day's work in Brixton, they invited him to come along with them if he wanted to. He didn't, though. So they dropped him off at the foot of Garnet Road.

He set off with his trumpet under his arm. He saw no one outside as he passed the farm. Tracy would be by herself this afternoon when the bus left her at the usual time. He walked on.

There was a For Sale sign out in front of the Valentine house. He supposed this meant that the insurance company had not yet called a halt to Eddie Shoop's claim.

Duncan stopped. He was thinking of going out back for another look at the burn area. But today, for some reason, he couldn't get himself past the image of the mummy, its smoldering eyes and gaping mouth and twisted limbs. So he made his way to the front door instead.

On the granite step he opened his trumpet case and prepared to play. Glancing in through the window, he was shocked to see only emptiness where the hospital bed had been lodged. What did he expect? It wasn't an object of sentiment to be packed up and carried off to New Jersey. Nor was it valuable like one of Astrid's "treasures" that Eddie might still be counting on to yield their double harvest.

Duncan peered farther and realized that the kitchen was pretty well cleaned out. He supposed the tape player and all those scratchy recordings had been trashed. Never mind, he thought. There would be a live performance for Astrid.

Raising the trumpet, he pressed his lips to the mouthpiece while his fingers found the notes. *When the saints*, he played. *Oh, when the saints go marching in …* The song blared at full pitch, just as Astrid, admittedly no saint, had requested. It didn't matter if he skipped a beat or if the trumpet squealed like a rabbit on the run. He was alone here on Astrid's front step.

Then from across the valley a cow trumpeted back. Others on the hillside where the dry cows were kept took up the call, bellowing in shrill, insistent chorus that sounded at once commanding and plaintive. Astrid would approve, he thought. She liked a vocal audience.

Duncan blew a coda. The cows returned his song, their chorus more muted now as, one by one, they dropped their heads to graze.

Not a bad sendoff, he thought, his fingers still clasping the trumpet. He nodded at the empty space beyond the glass and at his own reflection. A brassy sendoff for them both.